A PICTURE TELLS A THOUSAND LIES

A PICTURE TELLS A THOUSAND LIES

CLAIRE
OLIVIA

Book Cover by David Prendergast
First edition 2024

Paperback ISBN 979-8-9920952-0-3
Ebook ISBN 979-8-9920952-1-0

For Brian
who got me started.

CHAPTER ONE

MARCH 2022

Christie Hunter swiveled around on her office chair to face the window where she observed small snowflakes beginning to fall outside. Her phone vibrated on her desk due to a notification from a local news app. She glanced down and read the headline. *The worst snowstorm in twenty years is expected to hit Milwaukee on Wednesday evening. Widespread disruption to roads, businesses and schools is expected.*

That's tonight, thought Christie. So that must be the reason that Sandra, the Plant Manager at the Belle Corporation aerospace manufacturing plant, just emailed me and the senior leadership team about an immediate emergency meeting. Christie was not part of the team at Belle Corporation, but had been working there for three months as a Safety Consultant to help improve safety performance after an unexpectedly high number of accidents during the previous year. The company put strong emphasis on safety and therefore she often attended senior leadership meetings.

She felt gleeful as she thought of the forthcoming snow. It made her nostalgic about childhood days when school had been cancelled and she had joined her brother for hours of sledding until their faces were raw from the cold. Afterwards they would go home to mugs of steaming hot chocolate and warm cookies made by her mother. As an adult, she had also rejoiced in work closures that resulted in an unexpected day off—that was, until recently, when the Covid pandemic had made everyone proficient at working remotely. Christie shook her head, her long dark ponytail swishing across her back, as she brought herself out of her snow-related daydream. She made her way down the corridor and into the conference room.

The leadership team was small due to the plant only having one hundred and fifty employees. It consisted of Sandra Delaney the Plant Manager, Paul Merton the Production Manager, Jack Newbury the Safety Manager, and Cindy Lester the HR Manager. Sandra and Paul were already seated around the large oak table. Cindy arrived a few minutes later. She appeared distracted as she stared intensely at her phone. She told the others that the snow must have already started in some parts of the city, due to the number of Instagram snow-themed selfies she had already seen. Jack rushed in shortly after, muttering apologies about being late and looking a little flushed. Christie watched them all with interest. Despite their many differences and idiosyncrasies, they functioned well as a team.

Christie had majored in Occupational Safety and was now aged thirty-five and thoroughly enjoying being mid-career. She had been highly successful in the corporate safety world, specializing in manufacturing, and had a reputation for turning poor safety records around. Christie often helped clients decrease accident rates significantly within six to twelve months. Following her success, she decided to challenge herself further by hanging up her corporate hat and starting her own safety consultancy business. Her client base was steadily growing, and she knew that before long that she would need to hire a team to help with her ever-expanding workload. But for now, she was enjoying being her own boss and setting her own schedule.

Christie relished a challenge and turned eagerly towards Sandra to listen to the plans for the imminent snowstorm. At forty-nine, Sandra had finally reached the position of Plant Manager and was determined to succeed. It was her first time dealing with serious disruption to operations at the plant, and she was glad to have a competent team, plus the addition of a safety consultant, to help manage the situation.

"Thank you all for meeting at such short notice," Sandra began. "As you will know from the email that I sent at two-thirty, for the first time in the history of our manufacturing plant, we've received instructions from the corporate team to shut down operations immediately due to the impending severe weather"

"Wow, really?" asked Cindy, glancing towards the window. "I thought it wasn't exactly unusual to have snow in the Midwest, even in March? Yet corporate really want us to close?"

"Well, snowstorms can just appear out of nowhere, even in places that frequently get snow," said Paul, who had lived his whole life in Milwaukee. "But this one is supposed to be particularly bad. The safety of our employees is our number one priority, which is why we've already sent everyone home."

"Yes," Sandra continued. "Paul and I have already instructed all employees to finish what they're doing and leave as soon as possible, so that we can get the building locked up and everyone can get home safely. Everyone should be leaving now, but I wanted to spend a few minutes with you all to plan remote work during the closure. We'll use texts and emails to keep everyone updated about when we expect to reopen, but we will certainly close tomorrow, and possibly for the rest of the week. Does anyone have any questions?" She glanced around the conference room, but everyone shook their heads. "In that case, you are all free to go home. Be safe out there and we'll talk again in the morning."

Jack said, "Oh, just one thing before we all skedaddle. I think it's probably worth doing a sweep of the building to make sure everyone has got the message about the early closure and that people have actually left," Jack chuckled as he continued. "You know how some of our folks are__they never want to leave this place, even on holidays."

"That's a good point, Jack," Paul said. "There are some 'lifers' here who never like taking time off. Seriously Christie, we've even had some employees try and come in on Christmas Day, despite the plant obviously being closed." Christie smiled and nodded politely. She had also known similar situations where work was everything to some people, and they found it hard to cope with mandated closures.

Jack looked thoughtful as he said, "It might be worth checking the outside areas too. Some of our employees like to take their cigarette breaks in areas where they're not supposed to smoke, so it's possible some may not have got the message."

"Really?" asked Sandra, looking unimpressed. "I thought they had stopped doing that, since we installed a smoking shelter at the front of the building?"

"Oh, the situation has definitely got better," Jack said, "but some still sneak around the back of the building occasionally to avoid walking all the way to the front of the building, especially if it's raining or snowing. Anyone want to join me checking?"

"I will," Christie said. She admired Jack's work ethic and thought he was right about to check on the employees. She shuddered at the thought that someone could get locked in. She looked at the clock hanging on the wall and noted that it was three o'clock. It therefore wouldn't be long before the snow was forecast to start. Jack nodded and smiled appreciatively before asking, "Who wants to take the shop floor and who wants to check the outside of the building?"

Paul said, "It makes sense for me to check the production floor. After all it's my people who work there. Maybe you could join me, Sandra? We can swing by the maintenance shop too and let Billy know to tell his people to leave." Sandra nodded in agreement. "Actually, is Billy even here today? I haven't seen him." Billy Carter was the maintenance supervisor.

"Yes, I saw him this morning. He said he had a machine to fix which was likely to take most of the day, but he also had hazardous waste materials to deal with. He could still be around somewhere," Jack replied.

"Actually, I just saw him before coming to this meeting," Christie replied. "He told me that we're closing and that employees were leaving, so he must have already got the message."

"Okay, great," Paul said. "So that leaves outside for Jack and Christie. Sorry you get the colder option," he added, laughing. Cindy volunteered to check the offices to ensure that the administrative employees had left. Jack and Christie briefly headed back to their respective offices, gathered their laptops, files and other things for working from home, and then headed outside. They started at the front of the building in the parking lot, where the outdoor lights were flickering intermittently, and saw that most people had left.

"They don't need telling twice that they can go home early," Christie said, chuckling. From there, they headed along a path at the side of the building towards the end of the perimeter. No one was around. It was unusually quiet, and the snow fell in small flakes landing gently on the path in front of them. Passing a small window at the side of the building, they glimpsed Paul and Sandra in the distance inside the factory completing their checks. They noticed a fire exit door at the side of the building, propped open with a fire extinguisher.

"Ugh," they both exclaimed at the same time. They had only told production employees two days ago not to do this, as it violated fire safety regulations and caused a security risk. However, the employees had argued that the welding area got very hot inside, even in mid-winter, and they needed fresh air to help cool down.

"Let's walk to the end of the building and close the door on the way back," Jack said. The air was bitterly cold and gray clouds loomed overhead, threatening to bring heavier snow at any moment. They carefully walked towards the factory boundary that bordered a shooting range called the Smokin' Barrel. It was here by the fence that employees used to like to smoke, until the new policy prohibited smoking anywhere except the new smoking shelter.

There was only an inch of snow on the ground, but it was icy underneath, and although it was only just after three o'clock, it was already getting dark. Christie glanced back towards the building and noticed the lights flickering ominously. She shivered and wondered if the storm was going to cause a power outage. She would be glad to finish these checks and get out of here. Christie thought of the comfort and safety of being at home with her husband, getting a fire started, and spending a cozy evening inside. She checked her phone and grinned when she saw her husband had texted her.

Heard about the storm coming in? Are you heading home soon? It was followed by a kiss emoji.

She knew he worried about her safety, partly because he was her husband and partly because he was a police officer, and ever the cop, she knew that was his way of gently instructing her to head home, but she didn't mind. She replied, *Yes, heading home shortly. Can't believe how dark it is at only three-fifteen*, with a kiss emoji.

The wind was howling, and snow was starting to fall more heavily than when they had left the building minutes before. They were now approaching the very end of the factory exterior and saw that there was no one there.

"Well, it looks like everyone left," Jack said, looking relieved, especially because there were no illegal smokers out here.

"Yes, I'm sure they were glad to get out of here," Christie agreed. But as they got nearer to the end of the building, they both stopped and stared ahead. Something looked out of place. To their right was a small outdoor building where hazardous waste, such as used oils and chemicals, were stored until they were disposed of. Through the thick falling snowflakes, they could just about make out a reddish-brownish pool of liquid near the corner of that building. Christie frowned. Surely there were enough existing safety issues at this plant without adding an oil spill to the list of things that needed to be fixed?

Was it oil? It was hard to tell. She squinted through the snow and edged closer. Maybe it was paint or some chemical. She really hoped not, knowing that there were several stormwater drains in this area. But something was nagging at her. Something didn't feel right. The hazardous waste storage room was inspected weekly and was usually in good condition.

Surely someone hadn't illegally dumped something toxic in this area? She shook her head as thoughts of environmental concerns whirred through her mind. The clean-up, the reporting, the cost of re-training employees, the company's reputation. Now she was feeling a mixture of disappointment and anger building. She was certainly glad that managing safety at this plant wasn't her full-time job. She liked and respected Jack and knew he had his work cut out here. They looked at each other, their faces mirroring confusion.

"Is that some kind of spillage?" he asked.

"My thoughts exactly," said Christie. "Let's take a closer look."

They walked around the corner, determined now to identify this substance, but they both froze as their minds tried to make sense of the horror of what lay before them. The door to the room was usually locked but was currently wide open and swinging in the wind. Just inside the doorway was a body, partially covered in snow.

"Jack, what's that? Is that…" Christie shrieked.

"Oh my God," Jack cried at the same time. "What? What's happened? What the hell?"

The reddish-brown color was now much darker, a deeper shade of crimson, blood coming from a body that lay prone at an unnatural angle, limbs sprayed. Christie screamed, but the sound got lost in a gust of wind that howled around her. She couldn't make sense of what she was seeing.

Her mind raced with how wrong she had been in her assumption that it was some kind of spillage. She now realized that he shouldn't have assumed anything, but oh how she wished she had been right. The realization that something terrible must have happened made her feel weak and helpless, but at the same time knew she had to keep calm. Jack ran over and knelt by the side of the body, gently tilting the head backwards to open the airway and check for signs of breathing.

Christie took in the scene before her. The atmosphere was eerie, and she felt like a bomb had gone off and everything was moving in slow motion. She could see the victim had not dressed appropriately for the weather—wearing a beanie and scarf, but no coat—and she recognized the clothes and knew who the body belonged to.

Jack was yelling over the wind, "Christie, go and get help. There may still be someone in the building. Go and see if Sandra is still here. She'll know what to do."

Christie felt as though Jack's voice was coming from far away, as if the words were being heard underwater. "Is, is he dead? Is there anything that can be done?"

"I'll try CPR," Jack said. His hands shook as he spoke. "He's not breathing, I think it's too late, it looks like a gunshot wound to the chest, but I have to try. I have to do something. I'll start CPR. Call 911. Tell them what we've found, and head to the front of the building so the emergency responders can locate us."

Christie reached into her pocket and retrieved her phone. She dialed 911 and provided details of the emergency as she watched Jack attempt CPR. He leaned his face down towards the victim's face, delivered two breaths, then began chest compressions. He shook his head as if he knew his attempts were futile but didn't want to give up. He worked methodically, oblivious to the large snowflakes that were falling on top of him and the biting wind that engulfed them. Christie noticed the mechanical movements of the chest rising and watched Jack take off his jacket to stem the bleeding which was coming from the chest. She felt numb and was glad Jack was there to take charge.

Again, he yelled over the wind, "Christie, seriously, just go! Go to the front of the building to wait for the ambulance because the first responders won't see us back here." Christie jumped and nodded mutely. She ran towards the front of the building as carefully as she could without slipping. As she made her way along the side of the building, she noticed through the small window at the side of the building that it was dark inside, with a faint glow. Years of working in safety meant that she knew that the dim light was emitting from the building's emergency lights. If they were on, then the power would have been knocked off by the storm. *Damn*, she thought.

She reached the fire door that had been propped open earlier and planned to duck in there and run through the factory in search of help, but the door was now closed. *What the heck? It was literally just a few minutes ago that they had seen that door open.*

A shiver crept down Christie's spine as she realized that someone must have closed it within the last few minutes. Someone who may have seen her and Jack out there. Who could it have been? Most people had gone home. Was there a crazy murderer on the loose?

Suddenly there was a small bang. Christie jumped and let out a small scream. She knew the situation was making her more jittery than usual, and although that sound had been faint, almost muffled, it sounded like a gunshot. Christie had never felt so alone and so scared. But she didn't have time to worry about that now. She resisted the urge to run back to Jack and remembered what he had said about the emergency responders needing to locate her. She knew she had to get control of her fear, and common sense told her that the bang most likely came from the shooting range next door.

She was about to continue running towards the front of the building when she heard the swift opening of the fire exit door, and a figure stepped out into the darkness.

CHAPTER TWO

THREE MONTHS EARLIER

"Twelve serious accidents in three months at this plant!" exclaimed Mr. Ron Giles, Belle's Corporate Regional Safety Manager.

Jack sank a little into his chair. The moment that he had been dreading since the start of the meeting had undoubtedly arrived. Due to the lack of progress with safety improvements over the last year, and the marked increase in accidents over the last three months, corporate leadership had sent in the Midwest Regional Safety Manager to meet with the leadership team at the Milwaukee plant and agree upon improvements.

The December wind whistled outside the building, and the gray skies threatened snow. It was, in fact, a typical winter in Milwaukee. Ron Giles was one of eight Regional Safety Managers at Belle Corporation. His responsibility for the safety of employees extended across six manufacturing plants in the Midwest, and while the last five years had seen good improvements to safety programs overall, the plant in Milwaukee had troubled him, despite the plant possessing mature safety programs and an excellent on-site Safety Manager.

"Would you like to give an account of the accidents and plans for improvement, Jack? Keep it brief." Jack cringed inwardly, as did most of the other managers, as they all hated to be put on the spot, especially when their areas of responsibility were being scrutinized and they had to answer unfavorably.

"Well, while we are all aware that the Milwaukee plant has the highest number of accidents in the Midwest Region -," Jack began.

"In the organization too, right?" interrupted Cindy Lester, and she smiled sweetly. Cindy was the new Human Resources Manager at Milwaukee, and although she rarely meant to cause offense, she could be infuriating at times. She had joined the team in Milwaukee at short notice the previous fall and was known for her obsession with taking selfies for her Instagram account.

"Um, that's correct," replied Jack, doing his best to remain undeterred. "Last year we had four employees fracture bones due to slips, trips, and a fall from a ladder. There was also a case of eye irritation from exposure to a chemical, two severe lacerations from material falling from racking, two muscle strains and two joint sprains from lifting heavy items, and one case of minor poisoning from inhaling welding fumes. Full investigations were completed for each incident and corrective actions were implemented."

"And the causes of these accidents?" asked Ron, gesturing impatiently with his hands.

"Mostly a combination of the inexperience of new production hires, and the pandemic resulting in a decreased awareness of hazards in the workplace among office employees, as many of them now work remotely."

"Anything more tangible?" asked Ron.

"In some cases, risk assessments were not always completed or updated. Sometimes training wasn't followed. In the case of the eye irritation and the inhalation of welding fumes, the correct personal protective equipment was not worn," replied Jack.

"Hmm, well it's a trend that needs reversing, that's for sure. The safety metrics have got increasingly worse, so something needs to be done promptly."

Jack groaned inwardly. If he heard the word 'metric' once more during this meeting, he might be tempted to throw something across the room. He was reminded of the time he worked for a corporation called International Team Mechanics where employees had secretly joked that, due to the laser sharp focus on performance metrics, that the company name abbreviation, ITM, stood for 'Improve The Metrics.' Little did he realize at the time that all corporations were the same.

It was days like today where he missed his years serving in the U.S. Army. At least there, he hadn't been responsible for metrics. But no, he couldn't think of those times now. He had come so far since then. The explosions, the bombs, the loss of life. Jesus what was he thinking? He'd rather sit in a painful meeting like this any day than go through that again.

"Jack is one of the best Safety Managers at Belle Corporation. He has extensive experience in both safety and manufacturing operations and has put many new programs and improvements into effect during his tenure," Sandra said, interrupting his thoughts and attempting to come to his rescue. Jack smiled at her gratefully. The managers didn't always agree with Sandra, but they knew she had their backs. She was protective of her team and would defend them and treat them fairly. Jack explained that the Milwaukee plant planned to launch some new safety campaigns this year to re-energize employees and engage them in safety. He described some new safety training options such as blended learning, which offered a hybrid of in-person and online learning options.

"Yes, yes, that is all worthwhile, I have no doubt, but I don't think you're at that point yet," Ron said, somewhat irritably.

"What do you mean?" Jack asked in surprise, as he felt his action plan was substantial and the right way to proceed.

"What I mean is that before you decide upon what action to take, you need to understand why these accidents occurred in the first place. You need to ensure the investigations were of real quality and truly identified root causes. It is abnormally high for any of our plants to have twelve serious accidents in a year, let alone three months."

He grimaced as he continued, "not to mention additional minor accidents and near misses and who knows how many accidents that weren't even reported! Fractures, strains, sprains, lacerations, and poisoning! It cannot continue."

"Then what do you suggest, sir?" Jack asked as politely and calmly as he could.

"I suggest an independent review of the accidents. Bring in an external Safety Consultant to offer an independent professional review."

"Oh, I'm not sure that is necessary," Sandra said. "I mean, Jack is an excellent Safety Manager, and I don't want someone poking around our plant and treading on his toes."

"Nonsense! None of us are so good that we are beyond requiring help," replied Ron. "It would be a fresh pair of eyes to look at things objectively. An impartial view. They wouldn't be 'poking around,' as you put it. Their sole purpose would be to review your existing safety programs and assist with making improvements."

He continued to talk for another five minutes about the benefit of outside help and objectivity and eventually Jack and the leadership team conceded. Surprisingly, the more he talked, the more his suggestions made sense, and they found they could not argue against him. After all, everyone in the room knew that the right thing to do was to prevent more employees from getting hurt.

"Good—that's settled, then," Ron said, puffing up his chest

triumphantly, with the air of someone who had just signed a peace treaty with a particularly tyrannical adversary. "The Corporate Safety Team will assign a consultant to start with you in January, before the new year begins with more accidents." Then he muttered more to himself than the team, "Honestly how so many accidents of such a diverse range can occur in three months is a mystery. Quite a mystery."

CHAPTER THREE

Christie Hunter snuggled deeply into the fleece blanket she had wrapped herself in as she lay on her couch. There was a glass of wine within reach on a nearby table and the TV was showing the latest BBC version of *Sherlock Holmes*. She looked around appreciatively at her home, taking in the comfort provided by a well-furnished, medium-sized typical Midwestern house. Christie was enjoying the peace before her husband, Mike, got home from his work as a Military Police Officer in the United States Air Force. She knew that as soon as he arrived, he would playfully tease her about her obsession with British murder mysteries. *Foyle's War, Vera, Sherlock Holmes,* and anything by Agatha Christie were among her favorites, and they made her reminisce about her adolescent years spent growing up in

England. Christie's mother was English and had met her father, an American, when he was stationed in Suffolk with the United States Air Force. They had married in England and moved to Wisconsin. Four years later, they had Christie, and a year after that, her younger brother Jacob. When Christie was twelve, her father was deployed back to England, this time to the beautiful Cotswolds area on the Gloucestershire/Oxfordshire border. The family had moved to England with him for six years. Christie and Jacob had loved it there and would often joke about the quaint little villages and the funny English sayings. Jacob had decided to move back five years ago, and he loved living in England.

Somewhere between being caught up in modern-day London, Sherlock's unique analysis of the case, and the door opening and letting in the icy Milwaukee air, Mike Hunter returned home and looked affectionately at his wife before making fun of her current situation.

"Well, it looks like you've had a very stressful, busy day," he said chuckling and nodding towards the television. "Ah, good old Sherlock Holmes," he added, in an appalling attempt at a London accent, "When are they going to make an episode where the twist is that Doctor Watson is the villain?"

Christie rolled her eyes and said, "Oh please! How would that ever work? Doctor Watson is Sherlock's faithful sidekick. It would ruin everything to make him one of the bad guys. And for your information, Mike, I have been remarkably busy today and I'm taking a well-deserved break. I've written safety policies for one client, designed training templates for another, and typed up reports and recommendations following accident investigations. How was your day?"

"It was good, but I think you win for having the toughest day," Mike said, winking at her. "How about Chinese food for dinner?"

"Sounds good to me, as long as they will deliver in this weather." It had started to snow already, although it was not forecast for another couple of hours.

Mike laughed. "It's Milwaukee, they will deliver." Lola, their Yorkshire terrier, jumped around and pawed at Mike's leg, as if she could sense that food was being discussed.

"Okay, okay, I will feed you first," Mike relented, as he stroked her head and filled up her dog bowl. Mike began to place their usual order when Christie's phone rang suddenly. She noticed it was an unfamiliar number. She would've usually ignored it or assumed it was a scam call, but ever since starting her own business she was aware that it could be a client.

"Hello, this is Christie Hunter," she answered.

"Good evening. I'm sorry to call you outside of regular business hours. My name is Ron Giles and I'm calling from Belle Corporation with regards to safety consultancy services."

Christie was about to say that regretfully she didn't have the capacity to take on more work at the moment, but there was something in the gentleman's tone that stopped her. *Not exactly desperation* she thought, *but nevertheless something urgent, something intriguing.* She figured she may as well hear what he had to say.

Ron Giles regaled Christie with the account of the past three months at the Milwaukee plant and the need for improvements. Christie hesitated. She knew of Belle Corporation, the country's leading manufacturer of aerospace engine components. It was well known that the company had an excellent reputation for customer satisfaction, employee retention and most importantly safety. Although it would be great to work alongside highly reputable individuals, Christie was yet to be convinced of the need for her services. After all, they had a safety manager and put great emphasis on strong performance. It therefore seemed likely that their own team could fix their problems without external help.

She was about to say as much, when Ron interrupted her thoughts and explained that the safety manager was good and had tried various improvement methods, but to no avail. That piqued her interest. In that case, maybe she could provide him with some additional training, a fresh pair of eyes to review things, and some mentoring. This could be quite an easy job and might not take up too much of her time.

"Okay Mr. Giles, I accept."

"Oh, that is great news, Christie, and please call me Ron. I have heard wonderful things about you from former colleagues of yours and the testimonials on your website are excellent. Certainly, your reputation precedes you, and I look forward to working with you."

Christie blushed at the compliment. "Thank you, Ron. Belle is a great company, and I look forward to working with you too." Christie hung up and filled Mike in on the conversation.

"Sure, this isn't too much for you?" he asked. "I know you are pretty busy with other clients at the moment."

"No, I think it will be fine and actually, I think I will enjoy Belle Corporation. It's unusual for them to hire a safety consultant, as they normally have good safety people of their own, so I'm intrigued. I think it will be an experience unlike any other."

Christie had no idea just how right she was about that.

CHAPTER FOUR

A week later, Christie dashed from her car to the entrance of the Belle Corporation plant with minutes to spare for her nine o'clock meeting with the Plant Manager. She was never late and cutting it fine like this irked her. But traffic had been especially bad on I-41 that morning as the result of an accident.

The day had started off so well. She had left early to allow plenty of time for her journey, as she always did when going somewhere new. She left home, her SUV warming up nicely and had even built in enough time to stop at her favorite lakeside café, The Cinnamon Swirl, to buy a coffee, which was now carefully placed in the holder next to her seat.

She was dressed in a gray pant suit with a light blue blouse, her long dark hair tied back in a ponytail. She did not want to appear too formal, but neither too casual; she knew how important first impressions were. She felt confident and excited about her new assignment as she hit the road, listening to her current favorite true crime podcast about murderesses in the Victorian era.

This episode was a particularly sinister one, as the murderess had carefully placed poison inside chocolates and even tried to suggest the manufacturer of the chocolates was the responsible party. She was enthralled and totally captivated by the plot and how the villain had been caught, but her thoughts were interrupted by a phone call from Mike.

"Hey, you," she answered on hands-free. "Everything okay?"

"Yep, just thought I'd call to wish you luck on your first day with your fancy new client."

"Aww, thanks honey," Christie replied.

"Oh, and to remind you that I have to work late, so could you please pick up some dog food for Lola." *There it is,* thought Christie, chuckling to herself. *More like he forgot to buy some at the store yesterday.*

"Sure thing," she said. "Got a busy day ahead?"

"Yeah, I think we've got an inspection. In fact, the Wing Commander mentioned—"

"Wait, sorry Mike," she said cutting him off, "It looks like the traffic is really bad up ahead. Hmm…I think there must have been an accident." She braked gently as the other cars in front slowed down. She looked out of the window to her right as she slowly passed the two vehicles involved. Just like every other driver, she slowed down to get a good vantage point of what had occurred.

"Everything okay?" Mike asked, and she could hear the slight anxiety in his voice.

"Yeah, I'm just trying to look now."

"You safety people always have some kind of morbid interest in accidents," Mike teased.

"I do not!" she exclaimed defensively, but laughing at the same time. "I just want to see what happened and if anyone needs help." This was not because Christie had some macabre interest in road traffic accidents. Safety and accident prevention were lifelong passions of hers, so any little piece of information she could learn from, she welcomed. Christie loved the investigative part of her job. There was nothing so satisfying as putting the pieces of a puzzle together, to satiate her curious mind and solve the mystery so the world may be a better, and safer, place.

This morning's accident, however, looked like a run-of-the-mill minor accident where one car had rear-ended the other. All involved appeared to be uninjured, standing on the roadside exchanging what, she was undoubtedly sure of, were insurance details. One thing Christie noticed however, was another vehicle a little further ahead, undamaged. The driver had bent down tocheck on those involved, his phone in one hand, and a first aid kit in the other. It appeared that he was taking charge of the situation.

Christie smiled appreciatively and thought how despite the cynicism of so many, there were good people in the world who stopped to help others in their time of need. Christie remembered a time when she had done this herself when living in England. The combination of rainy English weather and narrow rural lanes had caused a driver to crash into a wall and Christie had stopped, called the emergency services, and comforted the driver until help arrived.

"It looks good Mike. I think everyone is fine. Anyway, I better go. Have a good day. I love you."

"Love you too," said Mike, hanging up. Christie left the interstate and turned right onto a small road. She followed it for ten miles. She noticed that the view was bleak out here with a few industrial buildings scattered around, a gas station with a small café attached called 'The Last Mile," and the Smokin' Barrel, a shooting range just behind Belle Corporation. She saw the impressive factory ahead and turned into the parking lot.

The large building dated from the 1940s and had a generous size parking lot with three flags out front. One was the flag of the United States of America, one was the Wisconsin state flag, and one was a pale blue flag with the Belle Corporation logo printed onto it. Christie had spent some time over the weekend researching the history of the Milwaukee plant and had learned that the factory was built during the Second World War to manufacture munitions. It had been acquired by Belle Corporation in 1950 to manufacture engine components for aircraft. Today their main customers were Boeing, Airbus and the United States military.

She parked and headed into the building via the icy footpath, the grit crunching under her feet as she observed the anti-slip efforts approvingly. It was bitterly cold outside and unexpectedly quiet except for the occasional tweeting of a cardinal, probably searching hard for scarce sources of food during these winter months. She could also hear distant gun shots in the background from the Smokin' Barrel.

Christie was greeted warmly by a receptionist with auburn hair and glasses, who requested that she sign the visitor logbook and then take a seat while she called Sandra Delaney, the Plant Manager. Christie marveled at the expensive leather chairs in the lobby and the beautifully framed pictures of the local area displayed on the wall in front of her, among photographs of senior leaders at Belle Corporation.

"You must be Christie Hunter," said a voice interrupting her thoughts, "I'm Sandra Delaney, the Plant Manager. Welcome to Belle Corporation and thank you for being here."

"Thank you. It's my pleasure," Christie replied.

"Please come through to my office and I will make you a coffee or tea before we get started," Sandra said kindly, leading the way. Christie hastily took advantage of the free caffeine, which would no doubt be necessary to get through the day. After the phone conversation with Mr. Giles a week ago, she was certain that it would be a long day ahead, meeting key people, seeing the plant, and reviewing existing accident investigation reports. Yet now as she sat in Sandra's office, the caffeine starting to increase her alertness, she found herself looking at Sandra, intrigued.

Sandra was not what Christie had expected. She was dressed in black pants and traditional steel toe-capped safety shoes and a long floaty green sweater. She had long hair wrapped into a bun and was wearing a pale blue head scarf. Her earrings were large gold hoops. She was dramatic and gazed at Christie intensely as she spoke. She couldn't be further from the corporate image of plant managers Christie remembered from the time when she worked in the manufacturing industry.

"So, Christie, tell me how you became a safety professional in the first place."

"Well, I was always interested in a career where I could use my skills to improve safety conditions for employees and legislative compliance for employers. I'm not one of those safety people who witnessed a bad accident and then wanted to save the day and ensure it never happened again. It was more about fulfilling a goal to help others and to help organizations succeed. A safe workplace is a happy workplace, and a happy workplace is a successful workplace. Oh, I suppose I do sound a bit cliché now," Christie said, laughing. "My dad was in the Air Force, and I was always fascinated by the inherent risks in his job."

"That's wonderful," Sandra replied, nodding encouragingly. "Oh, I just got a shiver down my spine, like you're supposed to be here, you know? Like the spirits sent you." Christie had just sipped her coffee and almost choked at the last sentence. She waited for the punch line, waited for her to laugh and then realized she wasn't joking. She suppressed a giggle and tried to keep a straight face.

"Er, sure," she said, although she wasn't at all sure what Sandra meant or what spirits had to do with anything.

"Someone, perhaps from the past has sent you," Sandra said, more to herself than to Christie. Her eyes were closed as she continued, "Yes, someone who has now moved on."

"Um, no, Mr. Giles from your corporate office sent me here," Christie replied, ever the realist and straight talker. When Sandra opened her eyes again, she was immediately back to normal, and it was like the conversation never happened.

"Oh, I know that, silly", she exclaimed and grinned in a childish manner, "I was thinking more of the bigger picture. Never mind, though."

Wow thought Christie. *Where did they recruit her from?* Despite Sandra' eccentricity, Christie once again got that feeling that there was something about this place and their situation that was fascinating. As she listened to the description of the accidents, their consequential injuries and their causes, and details of the safety programs that Belle Corporation had in place, she wondered again why so many should have occurred in a short space of time, despite a well-established safety management system.

Something here didn't make sense to Christie, and she was determined to get to the bottom of it. Was this the result of listening to too many true crime podcasts, watching too many detective shows, and reading too much crime fiction? she wondered. *I really mustn't view everything as a mystery*, she thought to herself.

Sandra's account of Jack Newbury the Safety Manager was excellent. He had been with the company for six years, during which time accident rates had steadily improved under his watch, with the exception of the past three months. *What then had recently changed?* Christie wondered. Naturally, the pandemic had brought about unexpected challenges and changes, but could that alone really account for an increase in accidents? She decided that she would start by requesting a tour of the facility and meeting the people who work there, especially Jack.

CHAPTER FIVE

Christie spent the morning with Sandra to understand the business operations and current challenges. Despite Sandra's bizarre references to spirits and things from beyond this world, Christie could tell that she was a very competent and thorough Plant Manager. She had a good handle on production, especially since she had only worked there for six months. Sandra showed Christie where the Visitor's office was located and told her that as they had few visitors at this time of year, Christie could use this office when she was on site. Once Christie had placed her things in there, Sandra introduced Christie to Jack.

Christie instantly knew she recognized him from somewhere but couldn't think where. He was six feet tall, with broad shoulders, blond, curly hair, and green eyes. As he they walked down the corridor he apologized as his phone started to ring. As he bent slightly forward to silence it, she recognized in that moment that he had been the guy at the side of the road helping with the car accident earlier that morning. It was the same movement he had made, bending down to carry his phone and the first aid kit on the scene.

"Oh, I think I've seen you before, Jack. Were you at the scene of the accident on I-41 this morning?"

"Yes, I wanted to ensure the drivers were okay, and as I always have a first aid kit in my trunk, I was able to attend to some minor injuries."

"That was very kind of you," Christie said. "I hope they were all okay and no one was injured?"

"There was one lady with a minor cut and some bruising, but the others were fine. With my safety knowledge and background in first aid training, I like to assist where I can," Jack said, proudly. Christie smiled. Jack then led her on a tour of the plant. He had a very pleasant manner and was clearly liked by the factory employees, who waved and smiled at him as they walked around.

She was impressed not only with the rapport that he had with the employees, but also his knowledge of machinery, manufacturing processes, and safety programs. He could just as easily describe the intricate workings of a machine that produced small engine components as he could talk about the safe use of forklift trucks and how they had recently been fitted with safety devices to lower the speed to prevent accidents.

So easy was his manner that Christie felt obliged to explain that she was not there to undermine him. But he brushed her comments away, smiling at her, and said, "Not at all. I welcome an additional review of our safety program and just want to get better. I'm hoping for a promotion this year and really don't want these accidents and poor metrics to stand in my way."

"That's great," Christie said. "I'm sure if you are aiming for a promotion, Belle Corporation is a great place to be, as the leaders seem committed to helping employees to develop skills and gain experience in order to progress successfully within the organization."

"Yes, I agree," Jack said. "It would mean a lot to me, honestly. I didn't have the easiest start in life. My dad was an alcoholic, and my mom just spent most of her time being afraid of him, so I left home at the earliest opportunity. I didn't go to college but joined the Army instead and completed my degree during my service. I've always worked hard."

They returned to Jack's office and Christie asked for an account of the recent accidents.

"They've been pretty bad, to be honest," admitted Jack "and I can't put my finger on why they're increasing. Maybe it's fatigue as a lot of our employees work overtime. Or it could be complacency, because many folks have been here for a while and know their jobs well, so they don't think that they will ever be involved in an accident. Most training is up to date and risk assessments have been completed for all job tasks.

It started with a series of slips and falls. A couple of people slipped over just out of nowhere, resulting in a fractured wrist and a fractured elbow. Then someone tripped over a wooden pallet resulting in a fractured finger and one maintenance guy fell from a stepladder, also causing a fractured wrist. Sandra says the place is cursed." He smiled feebly. Christie frowned. She didn't believe in curses or supernatural happenings of any kind, but she wasn't surprised that comment had come from Sandra.

Jack continued, "Then there were metal materials that fell from a rack and caused a cut above someone's eyebrow. A week later someone caught their arm on a nail sticking out of a pallet resulting in a deep laceration. Another employee accidentally splashed a chemical into their eye. They were wearing safety glasses, but they should have been wearing safety goggles, meaning they weren't fully protected at the time. There was a poisoning case after welding, due to not wearing a respirator. Then we had some muscle strains and joint sprains caused by poor lifting techniques."

"Can I see the accident investigation reports?" Christie asked.

"Sure," Jack replied, and he hurried to find them on the company SharePoint. He looked embarrassed and concerned. "Christie, if there is anything you can do to help us get better; I mean any advice you have for me, then I would really appreciate it."

"Of course," she said as she looked through the documentation. "Well, I think we can work together on some more thorough investigations. It doesn't look as though they've been systematically investigated. No offense," she added.

"Well, they've been done in line with corporate expectations, and Sandra was happy with them," Jack said defensively.

"Sure, but take this one, for example. *Slip caused by employee rushing.* I mean, that doesn't really tell us much about how to prevent it happening again. Why was she rushing? Why did that cause her to slip? I rushed here this morning but didn't slip, so there must be something else. What is the root cause of the accident? A wet floor caused by a roof leak that needs to be repaired, for example. Sandra is probably happy with this because she doesn't realize that there needs to be more depth. You need a methodology to draw valid conclusions. Then you can make accurate recommendations to fix the problems. She's looking to you to be the expert and lead on this," Christie explained.

"Yeah, I guess that makes sense," Jack said, rubbing the back of his neck. "I can absolutely work on getting better investigations put together going forward."

"Great, and I will be able to help you with that," Christie said reassuringly. "I think that will really go a long way to making things better."

Interesting, thought Christie, *I wonder if he has been biased during his investigations. Maybe he has tried to get the analysis to fit a predetermined outcome or has deliberately picked an accident cause that has a really easy solution, such as ensuring employees wear the right personal protective equipment.* She had seen this kind of thing many times in her career. She knew it was the downside to only having one safety person. No one else here knew the expected standard. But she was confident that she could help to turn that around.

Jack and Christie continued with their tour. The production floor was substantial, with a maintenance shop in the middle.

Jack said, "Actually, since we are speaking of accident statistics, it would be good for you to meet our Human Resources Manager, Cindy Lester. She deals with Worker's Compensation when we have accidents. We could swing by her office if you like?"

"That sounds great," Christie said. They went upstairs and walked down several corridors until they came to a large office with a window. Through the glass, Christie could make out a young woman, staring at her perfectly manicured nails and talking loudly on the phone,

"So, you see I said, well obviously he likes me, I mean ugh, like why wouldn't he? And then she was like no way, he's too old for you, and all time I'm just thinking, yeah, whatever, that's not exactly a problem when he takes me to the Four Seasons in Chicago at weekends. Then I told her how he just broke it off last weekend for no reason. I'm absolutely devastated, and she didn't get it, literally like no sympathy from a so-called friend."

Jack cleared his throat loudly as he and Christie stood in the open doorway.

"Oh, babe I've got to go, work stuff," Cindy said, quickly hanging up before her friend could answer her.

"Um, sorry to interrupt, Cindy, but I wanted to introduce you to someone," Jack said.

"Hi, I'm Christie Hunter the safety consultant."

"Nice to meet you," Cindy said smiling at Christie and shaking her hand. If she was embarrassed to be overheard on a personal call, she didn't show it. "I'm Cindy, the HR Manager."

"It's nice to meet you too, Cindy. How long have you worked here?"

"Oh, just a month. I recently relocated from Oklahoma."

"Wow, that's awesome. What made you move from the Sooner State?"

"It was just time for a change." Cindy flushed and looked uneasy, and Christie decided not to press her anymore. They exchanged pleasantries for a few more minutes and then Christie and Jack left.

Cindy felt headstrong and defiant. This was a new start for her, and she didn't want anyone, especially outsiders, to know why she was really in Milwaukee. She had left the past behind her and had to focus on what was to come.

After Christie and Jack left, Cindy checked her face in her hand mirror, moved her bangs to one side, and smiled confidently for a selfie. She immediately uploaded it to Instagram with the following slogans #readytostarttheday #HRlife #womeninleadership. She might be young and might have made mistakes in the past, but she knew she was smart and could do this job. She perched on the edge of her chair and looked around at the files on employee absenteeism, job interview questions, and employee satisfaction surveys. She would start the day by organizing her office and then review her calendar for the remainder of the week. She was feeling positive when Sandra entered her office.

"Hi Cindy, how are you settling in?"

"Good, thank you," she replied.

"Finding it perhaps a bit smaller and quieter than your old workplace in Oklahoma?"

"No, actually it's about the same," replied Cindy. "Can I help you with something?"

"Nothing specifically. I was um, talking to one of our production employees earlier, and he mentioned having some financial difficulties. Something about being in debt…awkward, I know." She pulled a face. "I wondered if you have any advice?"

"Tell him to come and see me and I'll talk him through how our Employee Assistance Program can support him."

"Oh, okay. It's just that I told him that I would personally respond to his query," said Sandra, with a smile that didn't quite reach her eyes.

"No need, Sandra, that's what I'm here for," Cindy replied, pulling her chair closer to her desk. "It's what you pay me for." Worried she'd gone too far, she quickly added, "So naturally I'm happy to help. You have plenty going on and this is within my remit. Who was it, by the way?"

"Oh Chris, Chris something, McAllister perhaps? Or maybe McAllen? I'm still learning everyone's names," Sandra said vaguely.

"Trust me, so am I," Cindy said, with a little laugh.

"I understand, we're both new, and I appreciate that it's your remit," Sandra said, then hesitated as if weighing up whether she should say more. Changing the subject rapidly, she said, "I'm curious what you think of the Safety Consultant."

"Oh, she seems pleasant. I'm sure it will be good to get a second opinion on things around here."

"Hmm, I'm just not sure why Corporate has to send people to poke around in our business. Seems as though Jack likes her, anyway."

"Really? I can't imagine him liking anyone until he gets to know them well. He seems like the kind of person who keeps himself to himself and takes a while to warm up to people. We both volunteer at the soup kitchen on Keswasha Street and when I see him there, he barely acknowledges me. Maybe, it's just me he doesn't like? "No, wait, that can't be it," she said, flicking her hair over her shoulders. "He seems almost a bit of a loner."

"I wouldn't say that, at all. He's quite active with the Boy Scouts, his church, and community events. You know, I just knew he was going to be a good fit when he moved here."

Cindy frowned. "Hasn't Jack worked here for six years? And you've been here for six months, right? So, he started before your time?"

"Yes, but that's not what I meant!" Sandra said, her voice slightly raised. "The spirits sent me a message saying that good things are going to happen, and those things would form part of my future. Well, there it was, Jack was hired, and I connected with him later, even if it was six years later. Timing is everything, you know." Cindy didn't know and felt immensely confused. She stared at Sandra agog but had to quash a giggle.

"Um, sure" she said kindly, "and hopefully we will get our accident rate down again."

"Now, now don't jinx it, Cindy!" exclaimed Sandra, looking panicked.

"Jinx it?" Cindy asked hesitantly, not knowing what would come next if she appeared too interested.

"Yes, you see during my last job at the Belle plant in Massachusetts, we worked for a whole year with no accidents. Imagine—twelve months and nothing, not even a cut finger! So, what did the safety manager do? She decided to celebrate by ordering cupcakes for each employee. Imagine four hundred cupcakes with pink frosting!"

"I think that sounds lovely," Cindy said, imagining the amazing opportunity for Instagram pictures.

"Lovely? The place was all decked out and it looked like a baby shower on steroids! Oh yes, she was a sweet girl, what was her name? Amrita, I think, but just guess what happened next? The very next day someone amputated their finger! Why? Because she jinxed it with her celebration."

Cindy stared at Sandra in horror, unsure whether this was some kind of joke. "Well, I mean accidents can't be jinxed, Sandra. There is always a scientific cause. That's terrible that someone lost a finger, but it was probably more to do with unguarded machinery than jinxing."

"I'm not so sure about that. It was jinxed, I swear it." Sandra swept across the room in a dramatic fashion and left.

Cindy felt relieved to be alone. She liked Sandra and respected her ability as a Plant Manager, but really couldn't get on board with the spiritual stuff being mixed with leadership advice. Then she stopped and thought about it more fairly. She had recently been promoted and perhaps felt insecure in her abilities to do the job, may even a little overwhelmed by it all. Although Cindy couldn't work out why as Sandra was certainly good at her job and production figures were good. Yes, there was definitely more to Sandra than meets the eye.

Sandra went back to her office. She had agreed to let Cindy transfer here from Oklahoma. The truth was she felt indifferent to the girl, but thought she could have her uses. *Yes*, she thought, *Cindy is young and impressionable, but tough and smart.* Furthermore, Sandra had learned something valuable from their conversation. Belle Corporation has an Employee Assistance Program that can help employees with financial troubles. That was certainly good to know.

CHAPTER SIX

As Jack and Christie continued to tour the plant, noisy machines churned away in the background. Large signs hung from the ceiling, proudly displaying pictures of the aircraft engine components that Belle Corporation produced. They were also posters displaying Belle's commitment to the safety of their employees, developing the highest quality of product, and delivering exceptional customer satisfaction. The production floor was neat and uncluttered, and materials were well-organized. Christie was impressed. Clearly the place ran like a well-oiled machine.

They had almost finished the tour when they walked past the boiler room and the Maintenance Supervisor, Billy Carter, rushed out. He was a man of fifty years, stout with gray hair and piercing blue eyes. His manner was gruff and a little standoffish. Jack introduced them and Billy hastily said hello. He seemed eager to get away, but Jack kept him there while he introduced Christie.

"You're a safety consultant?" Billy asked, his cheeks going a shade of pink. "Why do we need one of those exactly?" He narrowed his eyes at Christie, but rather than be offended, she found it amusing and intriguing. What did he have to hide? Before she could answer his question, the janitor, Daniella Rodrigues, also exited the boiler room and stood next to Billy. Both parties turned a shade of red and looked awkward. Christie sensed their embarrassment and felt mildly amused. An affair? In the boiler room? Well, she had seen a lot worse during her time in manufacturing. Jack also looked surprised, but not at all uncomfortable and she guessed he wasn't one for showing emotion.

"To help improve our safety programs and in turn, reduce our accident rate," Jack replied, taking the opportunity to return to their conversation.

"Ah, I see. Only I thought that's what they paid you to do, Jack? So, you're not up to par, eh? Well, I hope they don't find me a consultant from somewhere. I'm fine on my own."

"Ha ha, very funny, Billy. Ignore him, Christie."

"Yes, probably best that you do," Billy concurred. "There are plenty more interesting people than me around here, that's for sure. This is Daniella by the way, our janitor."

Christie said hi and introduced herself to the lady before her. She had deep brown eyes and her beautiful, shiny black hair, tied back in a long braid. She was about five foot two, and her dark skin was smooth and flawless. Christie guessed she was in her late forties. Christie was sure that she would never remember everyone's names, so she was relieved to see that maintenance employees and janitors, as well as production employees, had their names embroidered onto their uniforms.

"So, who else have you met so far?" asked Billy, suddenly appearing more interested in talking to Christie.

"Sandra and Cindy," replied Christie.

"Oh goodness" he said laughing. "Well, Sandra's into all that spiritual stuff and Cindy, well, I'm not one to tell tales, but she recently moved here because she's been dating someone a lot older—some stuffy old lawyer. I actually know the guy because he's a neighbor of mine, and rumor has it that he promised her that if she moved here, he would leave his wife for her, and they'd live happily ever after. So, move she did, but he didn't make good on his end of the bargain. Strange, combination really—he's as boring as you can get. I can't imagine what they found to talk about."

"Oh, right, because I'm sure was dating her for his desire for intellectual conversation," Daniella said sarcastically. "Honestly Billy you are the worst gossip. Leave poor Cindy alone and let Jack and Christie continue with their day."

Christie smiled and said, "Well, it's nice to meet you, but I don't want to hold you up if you're cleaning."

"What?" replied Daniella, in confusion. "Oh no, I've finished the cleaning. I just need to remove the sign." She reached for the

'Caution – Closed for Cleaning' sign. Billy started to mumble about the boiler only working intermittently and causing problems, and how there were some leaks in there, so Daniella needed to mop in there more often than usual. Jack and Christie nodded and walked off. If Jack was surprised by their awkwardness, he didn't show it, but Christie felt there was more to what they had just encountered than appeared at face value.

"Did you notice anything odd about that interaction?" she asked Jack.

"No, not really," Jack said. "Unless you mean Billy's demeanor, but he's always like that."

"No, I didn't mean that. I meant that Daniella was allegedly mopping in there. Yet when she came out of the room, she didn't have a mop or bucket, or any other cleaning items with her."

"Impressive detective skills, Christie," Jack said. "I can already tell that I'm going to really enjoy working with you. Truly, I think we will make a great team."

"Ditto," replied Christie, grinning.

Billy looked at Daniella in a defiant manner as they watched Christie and Jack walk away. He said to her,

"I'm not threatened by anyone they bring in. This place wouldn't last five minutes without me, and they know it. No one else knows how to fix these machines, deal with the boiler, attend to the leaking roof, and do everything else I do. Nope, they don't worry me at all. I don't think they'll be bothering us, so don't look so worried."

"Okay, okay, I hear you. I'm not worried exactly. I just don't want anything to change or get in the way of what we have going here. It just makes me kind of nervous when they bring someone in to look at improvements, because you know they will go poking around," Daniella said.

"There's no need to be nervous. Just keep doing what you're doing, okay? You do a good job, and everyone knows it. You don't need to worry," Billy said, reassuringly.

Finally, Christie was introduced to Paul Merton, the Production Manager. He was a pleasant and friendly African American man, and Christie thought he was easily the most normal of all the people she had met so far.

"Have you met everyone?" he asked.

"Yes, I think so," replied Christie.

"And no one scared you off? I'm impressed that you are still here," said Paul, chuckling. There was a twinkle in his eye and Christie warmed to him immediately, as she had done with Jack.

"Listen, on a serious note, Sandra may be a bit of a hippie, but she's harmless and has a thorough eye for detail. Plus, she's great with numbers. Cindy is young but is very smart and despite being easily distracted, she does work hard. Billy is a bit gruff but he's a workhorse. He's a good example of someone whose bark is worse than his bite. He's been here a long time and likes people to know it.

Daniella is very sweet and works hard. Both she and Billy are very good friends. Thick as thieves, those two. And finally, Jack here is excellent and has a real passion for keeping our employees safe. We welcome support, Christie. Please let me know if there is anything I can do to help."

"Thank you, Paul. That is very kind," Christie said. Jack thanked him too and they headed back to the offices to begin working on a new accident investigation methodology.

CHAPTER SEVEN

Christie returned home later that evening to the smell of steaks being grilled. Mike was outside carefully turning each perfectly seasoned steak as she slid open the patio door and joined him. They both enjoyed cooking, but Mike especially enjoyed grilling and participated in it all year round, as was normal in Wisconsin.

"Hey," Christie greeted him. "Smells great. Shall I get started on the side dishes?"

"Sure," Mike said, "but enjoy the wine that I've poured for you first." Mike was clutching his favorite IPA beer and had poured Christie a glass of White Zinfandel. "You look like you need it. How was Belle Corporation today?"

"It was…okay," Christie replied as she tried and failed to think of a more positive word.

"That good, huh?" Mike asked, grinning.

"Yeah, I mean it was certainly interesting. They have things they need to work on, just like all my clients, and they want me to be on site three days a week."

"Really? That much? Well, they're paying for it, I guess."

"Yes, they don't scrimp on safety. But it was so different from anywhere that I've worked before. The plant manager was totally not what I expected, and was a little crazy to be honest, but extremely smart and good with numbers. I can see why she has been recently hired."

Christie proceeded to tell Mike about the interactions with Sandra and her cherished spirits. "Then there's the HR Manager who was sweet and again smart, probably very good at her job, but I felt like she was hiding something. She's not from around here and seemed like she was holding something back.

The maintenance supervisor and janitor are quite possibly having an affair. Although he was very quick to tell me about how Cindy had moved here due to an affair with an older married man. The safety manager was overall very friendly, although perhaps a little defensive at times. Oh, and get this, he was at the scene of the accident this morning. Remember the one I told you about over the phone?"

"What do you mean? Was he hurt?" asked Mike.

"Oh no. He was actually providing first aid to the people involved."

"I thought you said that no one was hurt, though, from what you could see?"

"Yes, but I couldn't see everything, and he said there were one or two minor injuries."

"Well at least he wasn't hurt. A safety guy involved in an accident—now that would be ironic."

Christie rolled her eyes. "You know, Mike, none of us are perfect, not even us safety folks," she said sarcastically. "Accidents happen, even to the best of us."

"Well, he sounds like a nice guy."

"Yes, I think so and he definitely likes to be recognized for a good job, maybe because he's a little needy? I know you're going to say I'm being critical, but I can't help being a little wary of people who open up the minute you meet them and tell you their life story." She sighed as she imagined Jack as a child. "He comes from a pretty awful family background, left home as soon as he could, joined the army, then worked as a maintenance technician for ITM before joining Belle Corporation. I'm just not sure I needed to hear all of the background on day one."

"Christie, not everyone is like you. You come from a loving family that care about you. You fit in everywhere you go, and people love you. Your personality and your strong ability and determination to succeed are what make you likeable and successful. Maybe a little empathy wouldn't hurt?"

"Actually, I was going to say they weren't all bad, I just hadn't finished yet." She grinned. "The production manager was the only normal, down-to-earth one out of them all."

Mike laughed. "So, what do they want you to do? Anything safety-related, or just an assessment of crazy personalities?"

"Oh, just review accident investigations, which certainly could use some improvement, based on what I saw today, and spend some time on the production floor and make recommendations for improvements. It will be interesting and working there three days a week should balance out okay with my other workload, as most of that can be done remotely."

Christie began to prepare asparagus and garlic mashed potatoes as she continued to fill Mike in on her day. He in turn told her about his workday and then they sat down to eat.

"Wow, Mike, these steaks are delicious," Christie said. "I will never grow tired of your cooking." Mike grinned and returned the compliment.

"You know we still have some of your delicious cherry pie in the fridge?"

"Oh yes, the perfect dessert to finish off this amazing dinner," Christie said, smiling. Her specialty was baking, and she loved to make desserts, cakes, and cookies whenever she had the time.

When they had finished eating, they loaded the dishwasher and cleaned the kitchen, Christie's mind drifting to what her time at Belle Corporation would bring.

CHAPTER EIGHT

A couple of days later, Christie rose early, and after coffee and a light breakfast, she headed to her local public swimming pool. She had been a keen swimmer since she was a child and found that diving into the crystal-clear water and swimming for an hour before work soothed her soul, sharpened her body and mind, and set her up for the day. As she swam, her arms reaching up and ahead of her, she cleared her mind and thought about her first day at Belle Corporation.

This client was certainly different from her other run-of-the-mill clients. There was such a mixture of personalities, and she smiled to herself as she thought about how she would enjoy working there for the next few months. She got out of the pool, showered and dressed, and headed out to her car. She drove over to Belle Corporation, feeling motivated and ready to face the day. At the same time as Christie entered the building, Daniella was busy mopping the floor in the cafeteria. She smiled pleasantly at the scattering of early shift employees who were taking their morning break in the cafeteria while she mopped, trying as much as possible to stay out of their way.

Daniella enjoyed working here, especially as a means of regular income to support her recently expanded family. She had four daughters, and they were all married with children of their own totaling nine grandchildren. Her husband had died ten years ago, and she was reliant on her wages to keep her small house in the suburbs near Lake Michigan. She thought anxiously of how she we do anything for her family as she mopped furiously at the floor in a figure of eight shape. Faded memories of safety training from last year came back to her. Jack had taught them that mopping in the shape of a figure of eight was the most ergonomically friendly way to avoid a back injury. She smiled fondly, as she liked Jack and didn't envy his task of delivering safety training to tired employees, who just wanted to go home at the end of their shift.

"Hey, it smells different in here today," called one of the machine operators from a table where he sat chewing on his snack. Daniella didn't notice because her sense of smell had not been the same since having Covid four months earlier. However, she assumed it was a compliment as the pine scented disinfectant used for mopping the floors always smelled good.

"In a good way?" she asked.

"Hmm, not exactly no. It's like pine with a metallic smell, kind of oily. Is it a new floor cleaner?"

"No, it's the same as always," she said, shrugging. She finished mopping, placed the 'Caution Wet Floor' in position, and left the floor to dry. The cafeteria was always warm and the floor dried quickly. She took pride in her work and knew that there were no traces of muddy footprints from the snow outside. She left the cafeteria and continued to mop the adjoining corridor. Ten minutes later, when she had finished mopping that area, Daniella heard a scream.

She turned to see Jack and Christie running towards the cafeteria from the opposite direction. She went to see what was happening, carefully inching her way across the floor even though it was mostly dry now. Liena Chang, a middle-aged lady who worked in the factory, was sat on the floor clutching at her ankle.

"What happened?" asked Jack, his voice calm, but his face concerned. His eyes darted around the scene, and for a few seconds, he looked as though panic had set in.

"I was just walking towards the vending machine to get a drink, and I slipped and twisted my ankle. It was like my legs just disappeared from underneath me. It was so strange."

"Was the floor wet? Daniella, you were just mopping here, right?" Jack asked.

"About ten minutes ago and the floor is dry now," Daniella replied.

Jack turned to Liena. "Were you rushing?" he asked.

"No, not at all," she said.

"What about your footwear?" he asked, looking towards her feet.

"My shoes are standard company issued safety shoes, which have anti-slip soles," she confirmed.

"Hmm. Did you come in from outside?" he asked.

"Yes, I went to get my phone from my car because I left it there this morning," Liena said.

"That must have been the reason that you slipped," Jack said, looking relieved to finally have an answer that fit, "your feet are wet from the melting snow." He grabbed a first aid kit from the cafeteria shelf and ice from the ice machine, wrapped the ice with a towel from the kitchen area, and gently applied it to Liena's ankle. Liena looked at him gratefully and thanked him.

"We're lucky here, Christie," she explained, "Jack is always on hand to help when things go wrong."

"Yes, I see that," Christie said.

Jack felt uneasy. There was something about seeing Liena on the floor that had unsettled him. In his mind he'd been transported back to a time when he was a small boy, around nine years old, e, when he'd heard a bang from downstairs.

He tiptoed from his bedroom to the top of the stairs and peered around the banister. Everything had gone quiet, so he slowly and carefully made his way down the stairs. In the kitchen he saw his mother sat on the floor, clutching at her ankle.

His father was angry and drunk as usual. His eyes were red, his face flushed, his hair a mess, and he was yelling at his mother. She was always brave, and he could tell even as a young boy that as she clutched her painful ankle, she was trying not to cry. When they saw him standing in the kitchen doorway, they both yelled at him to go back upstairs. He remembered now that as a young child he could not understand what had happened. However, as an adult he knew all too well that his dad couldn't control his anger once he'd been drinking and often took that anger out on his mother. He understood now the fear on his mom's face was the reason he obeyed them and went back upstairs—fear that his dad would hurt him next.

The very next day he tried to make things better and tried to distract his parents. Jack had a gift for art. He had been painting late into the night and brought down one of his paintings in the morning. He presented it to his father and explained that he'd been painting a picture of the beach from a vacation that they had taken the year before. He remembered how proud he was of this picture and was certain that his dad would like it. His father had crinkled his nose and looked at Jack in surprise.

"Well?" he asked, "what is that supposed to be?"

"It's the beach," Jack explained, uncertain about why he had to explain this to an adult, who was surely much smarter than a nine-year-old child. "This is us eating ice cream, and this is the ocean and the sun," he explained impatiently, wondering if his father was being stupid deliberately.

He tossed the painting to one side, looked Jack squarely in the face, and said, "I don't need you to be doing things like this, Jack, do you hear me, boy? This is not what a real man does. When you grow up someday, you need to get a job that involves using your hands."

"Like painting?" said Jack earnestly, although still bewildered by his dad's words and not understanding why he was talking about men and jobs.

"No. Something that's manly, some kind of labor. Understood?"

"Calvin, please," his mother said pleadingly. "He's just a boy."

"Be quiet, Eileen! Can't a man have a conversation, father to son without you butting in all the time?" snapped his father, and his mother looked away nervously.

Jack remembered being disappointed that he got no approval from his mother either. He was furious, as well as hurt, that his older brother Donald excelled in everything he did – math, science, English and he had recently made the baseball team. Not that his father was particularly interested in either child, but his dad did seem to at least acknowledge his brother's achievements. But for Jack, it was different. Nothing he could do was ever good enough. He thought long and hard about what his dad had said. He decided that maybe he could seek some kind of approval and get some praise from him if he could just use his hands and do some kind of manual work.

The next day, he went out into the yard and stood on a bench to reach up for the wooden bird box that was hanging from a cherry blossom tree. His mom enjoyed watching the birds, and she had placed several bird boxes and feeders around the yard. He gently lifted the box down and took it into the shed, where he found his dad's toolbox. He rummaged through until he found a hand planer. Many times, he had watched his dad plane wooden doors around the house and thought that if he did the same to the bird box, then his dad would surely be impressed. Taking care not to slice his fingers, he gently planed away at the sloping roof of the bird box.

His dad suddenly appeared in the yard. He stood for a few seconds taking in what Jack was doing and started to scream and yell at him for going into the shed and taking tools without permission. Jack tried to explain in between yells that he was just trying to use his hands and do a manly task. The incident resulted with his dad throwing the bird box across the yard, narrowly missing his mom when she came outside to see what all the yelling was about. It was then that Jack realized that his dad did not care at all about his work or whether anyone got injured when he lost his temper.

Jack sobbed great big fat tears that ran down his cheeks, but this only seemed to anger his dad more. Hee ran inside and up to his room and cried and cried for the failure to please his father, and also for the little birds who may have been wanting to use the bird box that was now in pieces. The birds wouldn't be a family in their house any more than Jack would be part of a family in his house. He decided there and then that he would leave home as soon as he was able.

When Donald turned eighteen, he left for college and Jack suffered another couple of miserable years under his mom and dad's roof without an ally. His dad became more and more withdrawn and would often return home late at night, drunk. It was just Jack and his mother most nights, and she was too sad to talk to him.

As soon as Jack turned eighteen, he left home, telling his parents only that he was joining the Army and doubted very much that he would be back. His mother cried and apologized for not supporting him more, but it was too late. Jack's dad barely said a word and appeared, as usual, to be disappointed with his choice. And so it was that in 2002, Jack left for good. His home, broken and dysfunctional as it was, was the only one that he had ever known, but Jack had no regrets as he joined his local regiment. He never really enjoyed Army life, although he made a small number of friends, but friends were short-lived in the Army. He deployed to Egypt, Qatar, Germany and Japan before returning to the United States.

Jack had never felt the need to talk to anyone about his experiences in the Army. Like many, he had seen enough trauma and devastation to last a lifetime, and he liked to deal with these things himself. Now Jack's main focus in life was his work. He was happy for work to consume most of his time. He had little interest in romantic relationships. He had an odd fling here and there, mostly by meeting women in bars, but the flings never lasted longer than a weekend. His parents' disastrous marriage had been enough to put him off relationships or to pursue marriage. Jack liked to spend his weekends at the gym or at community events and to help with fundraisers organized by local charities or the church.

"Jack," Christie's gentle voice said, waking him out of his reminiscing. "How do you want to handle the accident investigation?" she asked.

"I'll meet with Liena's supervisor today and work with her to complete it," he replied. After resting and icing her ankle, Liena felt well enough to return to work after her break. She disregarded Jack's suggestion to take the rest of the day off.

Later Jack was in Christie's office, showing her the investigation report, to seek her opinion. Christie frowned as she saw that the root cause was listed as 'wet weather conditions'. It seemed no deep dive into root causes had been explored, which she found frustrating as they had only discussed the need to do this the other day. Jack was definitely going to require further coaching on accident investigations. She decided there was no time like the present to tackle this and asked Jack what he had ascertained during his initial investigation.

"I discovered that there are normally anti-slip mats in the cafeteria, but they weren't there today, which was strange," he said. "I guess they were removed for cleaning, although Daniella denied this. She said there had been no mats present when she began mopping."

"That is strange," Christie remarked. "Is it possible they were removed for another reason? Maybe they are being replaced?"

"Yes, that's exactly it. We do have contractors that come in and change them, but that is usually on a Tuesday and today is Friday. However, occasionally the days change."

"Okay, so that is definitely a contributory factor. What cleaning product does Daniella use?"

"Just regular industrial disinfectant. Why?"

"Some cleaning solutions can be more slippery than others," Christie said. "Is the safety data sheet available? As I'm sure you're aware, each chemical should have one."

"Yes, of course," Jack said. "We can go take a look if you want?" Christie nodded and they went to the janitor's storeroom. Sure enough, there was the regular disinfectant. They looked at the label and safety data sheet, but there was nothing in the ingredients that gave them cause for concern.

"Nothing unusual there," Christie said. But as she picked the bottle up, she caught a sharp smell and noticed a can of machine oil next to it. Odd thing to have amongst cleaning products, she thought, but she supposed maintenance may have placed it there. Satisfied that there wasn't much more to learn about the cleaning solution, she said,

"Well, I think we've done enough work for one day, don't you, Jack?" as they headed back to the offices.

"I couldn't agree more," he said, grinning. "This is how it's been with accidents happening so regularly. It's busy but I love my job. I'm just glad I was here today to help Liena. Let's call it a day. I'm going to finish the report, but I'll see you next week."

"Sounds good. Have a great weekend," Christie said, and with that she gathered her items together, climbed into her car, and tuned into the latest true crime podcast episode as she began her journey home.

CHAPTER NINE

Cindy tapped her fingernails impatiently against her desk. She was waiting for her computer to update, and it was tormentingly slow today. She took the opportunity to review her to-do list, which currently comprised of several sticky notes placed haphazardly across her desk and computer monitor. She looked at one where she had earlier scribbled the letters 'B' and 'D.'

Cindy was not normally one to take notice of rumors. However, the constant barrage of people at her door implying, hinting or outright saying that Billy and Daniella were having some kind of illicit relationship made her want to dig deeper. It would be entirely inappropriate if the rumors proved to be true, as Billy was Daniella's supervisor. Still, people could be very good at hiding things.. It was well-known that they were good friends, but several people had reported that they had been seen going in and out of the boiler room together and spending significant parts of their workdays in there.

One employee had walked past when they came out of the boiler room and had reported overhearing Billy saying,

"You know I think the world of you Daniella. Trust me, we'll be fine," to which she had replied,

"I do trust you, Billy. I'm just tired of hiding it." She hoped that whatever was going on between them, if anything at all, Billy wasn't making Daniella feel the same way that he made her feel.

Just thinking about Billy raised her blood pressure. He knew her reason for moving to Milwaukee and obviously felt some kind of power in holding it over her. Not that he had blackmailed her in any way. She actually didn't care if other people knew about her failed relationship, although she preferred that they didn't. He was more of an irritant, and she wished he would just go away. *I wonder if I could encourage him to leave, offer him a promotion to another plant, or just find some way to get him to go away for good,* she thought, knowing she was being unprofessional, but unable to help feeling that way. After all, Belle Corporation did not tolerate employees making others feel uncomfortable and it was her job to address the problem of Billy.

She continued to look through her list of items that needed attending to. "Oh, yes!" she exclaimed out loud, grinning to herself, "the charity raffle". This was an idea she had brought with her from her last plant in Oklahoma. Each manager was responsible for selling raffle tickets to their teams to raise money for the local children's hospital. Cindy approached local businesses for donations and accrued some excellent prizes, ranging from a free flight anywhere in the United States, to a fifty-inch TV, to boxes of chocolates, and many more delightful items. Relishing the opportunity to take her mind off Billy, she decided she would get away from her desk for a while and walk around the offices to sell tickets to the administrative staff. Hopefully by the time she returned, her computer would have finished with the updates.

She returned half an hour later with $200. She had only sold tickets to three people, but one had generously given her a $100 bill, and the others had given $50 each. She slipped the cash into an envelope and wrote "Charity Raffle Money" on it.

She was just about to place it into her top drawer when her computer flashed up with a notification that read 'Update Required'. *What the hell?* she thought, *isn't that what it was supposed to have been doing this whole time?* She groaned to herself as she grabbed her desk phone to call IT for assistance. There was no reply, so she jumped up hastily and went in search of Jim, the IT guy. Jim was almost retired and did this job more as a hobby than anything else. She found him fixing some of the computers in the finance office and explained the problem. He finished what he was doing and could barely keep up with Cindy, tottering along in her high heels as she marched back to her office. Within minutes, Jim sat at her desk and fixed it for her, confirming that the update didn't work the first time, so the computer needed a reboot. As Cindy stood waiting for Jim to finish, she glanced down and noticed that the envelope with the charity raffle money was missing.

"Oh, no!" she exclaimed.

"Is something wrong?" Jim asked.

"Yes, I mean not with the computer, but I had $200 in an envelope on the desk from selling raffle tickets. It's for charity and it's gone."

"Gone?" he asked.

"Yes, oh, how could I be so stupid as to leave it out like that? I feel terrible. It was in an envelope on my desk, and I put it there just before I went to look for you."

"Who would do such a thing? I'm sorry, Cindy. I hope you can relocate it," Jim said, leaving her office.

"Thanks, Jim. Me, too," Cindy said, but as Jim left the room an idea came to her. She thought of Billy's taunting face jeering at her. Anger surged in her until she thought she might burst. *I bet he took it, I bet he did,* she thought as she clenched her fists. *It's just the sort of thing he would do to get at me and make me look bad. Well, I will show him. I bet he won't expect me to say anything, but I'm going right down to his office now to confront him.* She quickly slipped off her high heels, changed into her safety shoes and jogged down the stairs and across the factory floor. She marched up to the maintenance area and straight into Billy's office, but to her dismay he wasn't there. *Ugh, damn him.*

She looked around briefly but could see no evidence of the money on his desk. Quickly she looked back towards the office door. The door was open and through it she could see that there were a couple of machine operators working methodically. They were focused on their work and not looking her way. In fact, no one seemed to have noticed her enter the maintenance workshop. She crept over to the door and gently shut it. She wasted no time in quickly opening Billy's drawers and snooping through. Nothing. *Hmm what did I expect* she conceded, *he isn't a stupid guy, he's not going to leave $200 lying around.* Just as she turned to close the last drawer, something caught her eye.

There was a catalogue at the bottom of the drawer for a tool company. *Weird*, she thought, *I know Belle Corporation has online accounts for ordering tools.* She knew only too well about the accounts, after once being involved in a theft investigation in Oklahoma where a maintenance technician had ordered tools for personal use via the corporate account. *So, unless he hasn't cleared out his drawers for years, which is entirely possible, it's unnecessary to keep hold of physical catalogues these days*, she thought. She reached down and pulled it out. Nothing looked out of the ordinary until she turned it over and noticed a slit had been carefully placed at the top of the back cover.

Gently she tipped the catalogue upside down and out fell two fifty-dollar notes and one-hundred-dollar bill. *Bingo*, she thought. Even though she suspected Billy of taking the money from her desk, a part of her was still surprised. She let out a sigh.

How could this day have gone so wrong? And then it went even more wrong. Footsteps were overheard coming straight towards the door.

Cindy turned towards the door in a panic. She knew she only had moments to think and hurriedly grabbed hold of the money and stuffed it down her bra. She felt sweat trickle down her back. She tried her best to look composed. Now that she had found the money, she wasn't going to give Billy the satisfaction of a confrontation or to let him know that he had rattled her in any way. She had taken back what was rightfully hers, and that would be the end to it. *Let the idiot think he lost it,* she thought angrily. Billy came in through the door with one of his young maintenance technicians, Joe.

"Cindy," Billy said curtly, "Can I help you?"

"No, not really. I was actually looking for you Joe."

"Oh, yes?" Joe said, looking surprised and a little alarmed.

"Yes, no need to look so worried. I have been working on improving our orientation program for new hires and I wondered if you would like to add a piece about the maintenance department?" Cindy was impressed with herself for making up such an elaborate lie on the spot and knew she now needed to ensure this work she proposed would happen. Joe looked at Billy who looked from Cindy back to Joe.

"Well, um, wouldn't that be up to Billy? I mean as he's the maintenance supervisor and everything?"

"Normally yes, but I am empowering employees other than

managers to get involved." Cindy said, "You know, not all good ideas come from supervisors," before launching into a speech about teamwork and opportunities. She hadn't meant to undermine Billy or, in fact, for any of this conversation to take place, but as she disliked him, she found herself not really caring.

She cringed inwardly, *wow, what is happening to me?* she thought. *I'm a HR professional. I never normally think this way or behave like this. Theft is serious and I should report it to Sandra, but there's something about this guy that riles me so much.* It felt personal after the way he had treated her. Billy looked entirely distracted, shrugged his shoulders, and grunted in a bored manner, "Sounds okay to me."

"Great, then I will circle back with you in a week or so," Cindy said as she made a hasty retreat from the office.

A couple days after the money incident, Cindy wondered why Billy had said nothing about the disappearance of money from his office. He must have assumed he had lost it or perhaps he hadn't even noticed that it was gone yet. Either way, it confirmed her suspicions that the money was not his, or there for legitimate purposes. If it had been, he would have reported its loss.

CHAPTER TEN

It was Wednesday lunchtime when Christie drove to the nearby café, "The Last Mile", fervent about both a change of scenery and a change of food from the Belle Corporation cafeteria. She ordered and paid for a grilled cheese and ham sandwich and a cappuccino and sat down on a hard, plastic bench at one of the booths. She noticed that a few Belle production employees were also taking their lunch break there, recognizing their blue shirts with the "Belle Corporation" name and logo, as well as their own first names, embroidered on the front. She smiled politely at the few that she recognized as she waited for her food to arrive.

She overheard parts of their conversation. It began with mundane comments about the weather getting colder and what they were planning for the weekend, but then she overheard something that made her sit up and listen harder. A couple of middle-aged men whose names she could just barely make out from where she was sitting were "Steve" and 'Eric" were musing over Liena's accident.

The man named Steve said, "It seems strange that Liena has never had an accident in all the time she has worked here. She didn't do anything unusual that day in the cafeteria, you know, she just walked over to the fridge like normal. Now if you ask me, there's something fishy going on."

"Like what?" the red-faced man named Eric asked. "Accidents happen, anyone can be affected." At that moment, Christie's food arrived, and she nodded and muttered a quick thank you to the waitress before continuing to strain to hear the rest of their conversation.

"Like there's a conspiracy or something among management. It's weird, these accidents just keep happening," Steve said. Christie sat still, unsure whether she should interrupt them and introduce herself but decided against it. She made a pretense of studying the menu in front of her as she hid behind it, slowly taking a bite from her sandwich.

Eric laughed, "Whoa, dude. I think you're getting carried away with the conspiracy theory stuff. Surely, we had enough of that during the pandemic."

"Maybe, but all I'm saying man is that it's weird, isn't it? Maybe they just make up all these accidents to add to their statistics, then they can look good when it gets better."

Seriously? Thought Christie. This conversation is wild.

"I really don't think they can make them up. Anyway, today we saw that Liena really did get hurt."

"Yeah, but what if they are in cahoots with that safety consultant? Like they tell her it's bad and they need her to fix stuff. Then she's getting paid a pretty penny and then they get their cut for bringing her in."

Christie decided it was time to make a swift exit. She put her menu down, left a tip on the table, and quickly went to the exit door, keeping her eyes firmly fixed ahead of her. *Wow, that was some crazy reasoning back there.* She thought. She was glad to be away from those men. But it was concerning to Christie that employees didn't have faith in the leadership team or the results of the accident investigation. She debated whether to talk to Jack about the conversation she had overheard but decided that it could wait for now.

Christie arrived back at the plant around one o'clock and noticed that Jack wasn't in his office, so she went out onto the factory floor to look for him. She walked past a few machines and smiled and waved at some of the operators. She was getting to know Belle employees well now, and they were warming up towards her. The atmosphere was busy but pleasant, and people were smiling and whistling as they worked. As she walked past a milling machine used to cut and shape metal parts, she stopped in surprise to see Jack with his sleeves rolled up, crouched down with a flashlight in one hand and a small wrench in the other.

"Hey Jack, what's happening out here?" she asked.

"This machine has been down since six o'clock this morning, so I figured I would come take a look and see if I can help to get it back up and running. It's not uncommon for chips to clog in the teeth of the cutter," replied Jack, beaming at her, clearly enjoying helping out.

"Isn't there anyone from maintenance available to help?" Christie asked.

"Billy is up on the roof trying to identify where the leaks are coming from, and both Joe and Graham are either busy with other machines or gritting the pathways due to the ice," replied Jack, keeping his eyes fixed on the problem part of the machine.

"And are you, um, qualified to fix machines? Not that I'm criticizing. It just falls outside the regular safety manager position," Christie said, firmly.

He grinned and said good naturedly, "No offense taken and yes, I'm qualified. I used to work as a maintenance technician at ITM in my last job. It was actually what sparked my interest in safety. I worked closely with the safety team there and became interested in their work."

"He's a huge help to us machine operators, and between us Christie, he often responds more readily to issues and does a better job than maintenance. We're lucky to have him," said the machine operator Katie, as she wiped oil from her hands.

"That's great," Christie said, but she secretly had her doubts. Perhaps if Jack spent more time on the job that he was paid to do, then safety wouldn't have taken a turn for the worse. But she reminded herself that all she could do was advise him. She wasn't his boss after all. People here thought very highly of Jack, but if Christie was Sandra, she would rein him in more. She made a mental note to talk to Sandra about it at a later point.

"It really is," Katie continued. "Especially given the near miss incident we had two weeks ago."

"What near miss?" Christie asked sharply.

"It was reported ma'am. I can assure you we followed policy."

"It's okay Katie, you're not in trouble. She just wants to know what happened," said Jack, reassuringly.

"Well, it was like this. I loaded the parts into the machine as usual and started it up when suddenly the machine stopped just for a second or two. Then it started up again but made a spluttering noise. Shortly afterwards a small metal part just flew right out and almost hit me square on my face. Good thing it's mandatory to wear safety glasses here.

Years ago, I worked in a small machine shop, and before that I used to fix up cars. I know what you're probably thinking, not a typical job for a woman, right? But I've always loved that kind of work, and my dad and grandad taught me all about cars from a young age. So anyway, back in the machine shop we never had to wear any personal protective equipment. My father worked in the mining industry and safety wasn't what it is today -"

"Thank you, Katie," Christie interrupted, before the history of safety standards in mining became the main focus of the conversation. Christie leant forward to review the maintenance records hanging in a plastic sheet protector on the machine. She could clearly see checks were carried out visually every day by the operators before the machine was used. In addition, checks were conducted by the maintenance team weekly, and they completed even more thorough inspections on a quarterly basis.

"Seems like something got jammed up," Jack said as if reading her mind. "A loose piece of metal probably chipped off one of the components as they were being fed through."

"Thoughts on how that can be prevented from happening again?" Christie asked.

"You're giving me that look again," Jack said.

"What look?"

"A look of disapproval, like you expect more from me."

"Yes, and I make no apologies for that, Jack. We need to get serious about preventing these accidents."

"That's what I'm doing out here now," he said, gesturing to the machine and his tools.

"I'm not talking about reacting to accidents, Jack. I'm talking about getting ahead of things, working proactively to prevent them. If a metal part was ejected from this machine, flew into the air and almost hit someone in the face, it clearly wasn't contained. That could have been a serious accident.

Katie was lucky this time, and even though she wears safety glasses, she might not be so lucky next time. It still shouldn't have happened. It should have been contained with a much more appropriate guard," Christie said, resolutely.

"I agree that the guard is insufficient, so I will order a bigger and more appropriate one. I know we also need to keep the machine well-oiled and clean, inspect and maintain it regularly. Operators are trained and wear the right personal protective equipment. I will also talk to Billy and get his input."

"Sounds good," Christie said, feeling more reassured.

Later that evening, Christie and Mike decided to have dinner at one of their favorite restaurants in the city, "The Lake House". They ordered a bottle of white wine and Christie decided on the seafood linguine while Mike chose the chicken parmesan.

"So, how are you enjoying Belle Corporation, now that you have been there for a couple of months?" Mike asked.

"It's good. I think things are definitely improving with more thorough accident investigations. The team members are a mixed bag, that's for sure. I mean everyone loves Jack, he's very popular, and I can understand why. He's approachable, helpful and always steps up when something goes wrong.

At first, I thought he had a great approach, but I've actually had to speak to him about not being so reactive and having a more proactive approach. I think he has good knowledge and experience, but maybe he's a bit lazy when it comes to the leadership and the administrative side of the job. It's been good for me actually, as I've learned not to take everything at face value, but to be firm when needed."

"How did he respond to that?" asked Mike.

"I don't think he liked it, to be honest. I think Jack is someone who likes praise and likes to put things right and be hands on. But hopefully, he'll listen to me and get better in time."

"Well, that's good, I guess. What about the others. Still a bit nuts?"

"A bit?" said Christie, laughing. "Yes, Cindy is nice but after her recent disastrous relationship, I'm not sure how much she really wants to be in Milwaukee. There's definitely some tension between her and Billy, the maintenance supervisor. He is an interesting character and a bit of a contradiction."

"What do you mean?"

"He works hard and is extremely knowledgeable about the machines and infrastructure and just about everything in that place, but he can be aloof at times too. For example, he knows how to fix the leaking roof but feels smug because his team members are the only people with that knowledge, so has no sense of urgency and sets his own schedule.

He has an extremely high opinion of himself. In fact, I think he's much smarter than he lets on, and he knows how much that place depends on him. He also seems to have some kind of hold over Sandra and the other managers, but I have no idea why. Unfortunately, though, he can be unkind towards others, mostly younger folks like Cindy, but never to Daniella, the janitor. They are very tight and she's sweet and very family oriented, but rumor has it there is something going on between them."

"Really? Wow. Such scandal," Mike said, laughing as he sipped from his glass of wine.

"I know, right? But why else would they spend so much time together and disappear into the boiler room? I can't imagine! I'm sure Cindy and Sandra are looking into it though. Every time they see me, they look so nervous, like rabbits caught in the headlights, and I have no idea why. I'm hardly there to investigate HR issues! Then there's Sandra who is great at her job but has her head elsewhere with her spirits and Ouija boards."

"I'm sure it's not your imagination, Christie. You have a reputation for being approachable and putting people at ease." Christie nodded as she ate her linguine, thinking about what Mike had said. He was right, most of the employees liked her as far as she could tell, plus she was hardly going to be there forever. She wasn't one of their corporate employees, so she was no threat to anyone. Yet, why then did it seem as though most of the leadership team, in addition to Billy and Daniella, were always on edge in some way?

CHAPTER ELEVEN

A couple of weeks later, after a refreshing morning swim, Christie arrived at Belle Corporation to begin another day's work. By now she felt settled there and was enjoying spending time with the employees and reviewing the safety programs. Jack and the others seemed to be responding more positively to the changes she had implemented. It was a particularly cold morning, despite the sun shining brightly.

Christie had now figured out the layout of the building and was confident to review things on her own without the dreaded feeling that she would get lost. The factory was on the first floor while the second and third floor were made up of offices and conference rooms. At the back of the building was a hazardous waste storage area, generators, dumpsters, company vehicles, and a storage area under a temporary structure for old equipment awaiting disposal.

This morning, Christie walked around the outside of the building, familiarizing herself with emergency exits and the hazardous waste storage room. Jack had given her the key to the room, and she slipped it into the lock and let herself inside. It was freezing cold and there were cobwebs hanging from the ceiling. She shivered and decided to make this a quick safety audit. She looked around and saw fifty-gallon drums of oil and chemical waste standing on secondary containment pallets, ready to catch any spills should they occur. She walked between the pallets, noting that the walkways were clear, and the emergency spill kit and emergency shower were accessible. She smiled and nodded to herself in approval. Jack and Billy were doing a great job in maintaining compliance with safety regulations out here.

Satisfied, she moved toward the door when suddenly she heard something. A scraping noise was coming from the back of the room. She turned suddenly, but before she could attempt to ascertain where the noise was coming from, the lights went off and plunged her into darkness.

Oh Jesus, she thought as she grabbed her cell phone out of her pocket and turned on the flashlight. She slowly edged towards the door, groping for the walls to guide her. She came across a small ledge and felt around it. *How strange,* she pondered as she shined her phone towards it. There was a tiny metal panel that was built into the wall and would have almost certainly been missed if she had continued to walk around in the light. She ran her hand across it and found a keyhole. What a bizarre thing to find in a room storing hazardous waste. *Still, it was an old building,* she supposed. Who knows what it was or why it was there? Her mind returned to getting out of here now that the power was off.

"Hello?" she called out. "Jack? Billy?" There was no reply, and she finally felt the door handle and turned it. It was locked. Fear gripped Christie, despite having a key.

She had only been in there for a matter of minutes and the light was off and the door locked. Was this someone's idea of a sick joke?

"Hello?" she called again, rattling the doorknob. She got out her key and placed it into the lock, but to her horror, it wouldn't turn. It felt as though the key was stuck. She wiggled it around and tried again, but it still wouldn't unlock. She looked at her phone and decided to call Jack. Christie trembled despite herself.

"Hey, Christie," came Jack's voice, "if you're wondering what I have planned for this afternoon, we have a review of fire safety to complete with the leadership team and I know it's not the most exciting thing but—"

"Jack, listen, I'm stuck in the hazardous waste room."

"What?" Jack asked, beginning to laugh. "How did that happen? Don't you have a key? Do you need me to come and rescue you?"

"No, I'm serious, Jack. I heard a noise, the lights went out, and the door is locked. Of course, I have the key that you gave me, but it's now stuck in the lock. It won't turn and I can't get out."

"Jesus, are you okay? Sounds like something from *The Shining*. I'll be over right away. Just take the key out, okay? I have a spare one, so I'll unlock it from the outside and get you out. I'm on my way now. Just hang tight."

Well, it's not like I can do anything else, thought Christie, as she removed the key. Christie heard whistling and then banged on the door. "Hello!" she yelled. Someone tried the doorknob, then Christie heard a key being inserted into the lock and it swung open. Billy stood there with a look of total surprise on his face.

"Christie! What are you doing in there in the dark?"

"That's a good question. Is there a power outage?"

"No," Billy replied, shaking his head.

"Well, the lights went off and the door closed and was locked. My key worked to unlock it from the outside, but wouldn't work to unlock it from the inside," said explained, just as Jack appeared, jogging over to join them.

"That's weird," Billy said, his face full of concern. "Let's see your key." He took it from her and tried several attempts to unlock the door from the inside. "It's an old lock and there's a certain knack to it. The problem is that's an old key too. See mine here fits better, still not great, but unlikely to have the same problem."

"Well, I recommend getting the lock and key replaced before someone gets locked in there again," said Christie.

"I agree," Jack said, as he tried his spare key and noted that it unlocked with some difficulty.

After the incident, Christie and Jack headed back to the offices. As they crossed the path to the building, Jack looked at Christie.

"Hey, I'm sorry that happened to you in there. Must have been a bit scary. Are you okay?"

Christie shrugged it off, "Absolutely. I'm not scared of the dark or narrow spaces or anything like that. I'm more angry than afraid."

"Why angry?" he asked, surprised.

"Look Jack, I don't want to throw around wild accusations or anything like that, so what I'm about to say must stay between us, okay?"

"Of course," he said, looking genuinely concerned.

"This may sound a bit ridiculous, but I can't help feeling that I was locked in there on purpose." Jack's eyes flashed and he stood still, turning to face her.

"Are you serious? Who would do that? And more to the point – why?"

"I have no idea. It just seemed a real coincidence that within a few minutes of being locked in there, actually right after I hung up from our phone conversation, Billy was there and opened the door, acting surprised."

"You're saying that you think Billy may have done it deliberately?"

"I have no proof, of course, which is why I'm only discussing this with you in confidence. But I've seen the way he treats people, especially women, except, of course, Daniella, but let's not go there right now. I don't know. It's just something we should keep an eye on. I'm not going to confront him because I have no evidence but, like I say, it's something to just be aware of."

"Wow, okay. I mean, I don't disagree with you that he'd be capable of a cruel prank like that," he mused thoughtfully.

"Oh, and another thing. Did you know there's some tiny metal panel against the wall in there? I'm not sure what it is, but it might be worth knowing about or asking if Billy knows."

"Really?" Jack asked, intrigued. "I had no idea. Although I have a bunch of keys that I inherited when I started here. There are one or two that I've never known what they are for. Let's grab some lunch now and have a look this afternoon and see if one of them fits."

Feeling content with full stomachs, they made their way back over to the hazardous waste storage room an hour later. This time, Christie was sure to prop the door open after this morning's disaster. Jack fumbled around with a set of keys.

"Sorry Christie, but neither of them fit," he said.

"What are you doing in here again?" said a voice at the door. They both turned to find Billy standing there.

"Just trying to establish what this metal panel is for," Jack said.

"Let's see," Billy said, pushing roughly past them both. "That used to be an old electrical box many years ago . But it's been disused for years and all the cables disconnected and removed. As it's redundant now I wouldn't worry about if being a safety hazard or anything like that." He walked away whistling to himself. Jack shrugged and appeared content with Billy's answer. But as they walked back to the main building, Christie couldn't help but wonder if what they had just been told was really the truth.

CHAPTER TWELVE

The following week Jack and Christie sat together in the Visitor's Office that Christie used every time she worked at Belle Corporation, reviewing the accident figures on the computer screen for January and February. They were pleased to see progress, as the number of accidents had declined compared to the previous year. Furthermore, the safety issues that were identified during recent investigations had now been resolved. However, despite this recent success, pressure was still being applied by Ron Giles to see even fewer accidents.

"I'm not sure what more we can do," Jack said despairingly. "It's so frustrating because I really feel like I've given so much to this place. We're steadily getting better but I'm just at a loss for ideas to make things better still."

Christie smiled sympathetically. "Don't give up Jack. We've all been there."

"Really, you have too?" he asked, looking surprised.

"Oh yes, any safety professional worth their salt has been through this. I mean if you work somewhere where everything is fine it's obviously great because no one gets hurt and that's the best case scenario, right? But you won't learn as much. What I mean by that is our failures are what shape us because we learn from our mistakes. I worked at a plant in Georgia where I inherited a mess. It took me about eight months to sort it out and decrease the accident rate. So, trust me when I say these things take time to fix. Safety is about building up a culture within a workplace where people are comfortable to report hazards and participate in resolving them. Ron knows it won't be fixed overnight, but I'm sure he is also under pressure from his supervisors to see better results."

"So, what was your secret for improving things?" Jack asked, smiling weakly.

"No secret. Just hard work, spending a lot of time on the floor speaking with employees to understand their concerns, tackling the highest risk areas first, and involving them in everything you do.

"You know," Christie continued slowly, "there is something that might be worth a shot. Something that really worked for me in the past."

"Really?" Jack asked. "At this point, I'd try anything. I feel I work hard, even though it's not always recognized, and I really want a promotion. Despite the current results, I feel like I deserve it."

"Okay," Christie said, excited to share her idea. "When I worked in the manufacturing industry, we did something called "Safety Week", which basically involved dedicating an entire week to safety. Each day you pick a different safety activity and get employees involved and engaged."

"Hmm," Jack said. "I'm not sure that Sandra or Paul will buy into that anything that takes employees away from production."

"True," Christie said, "But what about if we incorporate activities into productivity so there is minimal lost time, or we do some training which is mandatory anyway and won't involve a lot of time away from the shop floor? At the end of the day, managers need to be convinced that this is an investment in their employees and will ensure that safety improves. That in turn improves productivity in the long run. That's how we achieved it where I worked previously."

"I like the sound of that," Jack said. "So, what kind of activities did you do in the past? I mean, what are you thinking?"

"It's really up to you," Christie replied. "Some examples include first aid training, fire extinguisher training, things that you can make fun. You can also include some competitions, for example, a competition where employees identify workplace hazards. The person who identifies the most significant hazard, and offers a solution to fix it, wins a prize. We could look at retail vouchers or other prizes. I bet Cindy would be a great person to help with that. Then there are things such as a safety scavenger hunt where people walk around the building and identify the location of items such as first aid kits, fire extinguishers, emergency showers, eye wash stations and spill kits. Again, for those who find them all, they win a prize.

There's no end to things we can do. Maybe on the last day we could finish with a celebratory meal?" Upon seeing Jack's face she added, "Hey, I know it's Milwaukee in early March, so it's not exactly cookout weather, but we could do some kind of indoor celebration where we could still have hot dogs, burgers, maybe a pizza day, and announce the prizes."

"I love that idea," Jack said grinning. "Thanks so much, Christie. Honestly, I don't know what I would have done if you hadn't showed up here. You have helped so much. This is an awesome idea. Why don't we go and speak to Sandra about it now?"

"Okay, sounds like a plan!" Christie said, beaming. "I'm so glad that you're happy about this idea, as I'm confident it will go a long way to helping safety improve. I'm not saying that this alone will significantly decrease accidents, but it's a start. It gets people engaged and focused on safety."

After gaining approval from Sandra, Christie and Jack spent several days together planning Safety Week. Jack had kept his first aid trainer qualification up to date since leaving the Army, so it was agreed that he would deliver first aid training. He had recently discovered a website that specialized in first aid equipment, and he planned to purchase a lifelike manikin to make the training more realistic.

Billy was qualified to deliver fire extinguisher training, and he agreed to dust off an old presentation that could be used to teach people the basics around fire safety. He would also reserve an area in the parking lot for people to complete the practical part of the training by letting off fire extinguishers.

Christie spent some time drawing out scavenger hunt maps and identifying emergency equipment and other safety equipment. Jack worked on a safety quiz to test the operator's knowledge about machine safety. They also worked on designing a template for people to submit significant hazards and solutions. The leadership team were very supportive of the event, and everybody was excited. Cindy and Jack created some posters and displayed them around the building, as well as uploading a copy to the company's safety SharePoint to advertise the event.

It was agreed that on the Friday of the chosen week, the afternoon would be dedicated to having barbecue food and announcing winners from the Safety Week competitions. Ron Giles was also invited to represent corporate safety. Ron asked Jack to write an article for the company newsletter so that other plants could follow suit, assuming that Safety Week was successful.

CHAPTER THIRTEEN

Monday morning dawned bright and sunny with blue skies, despite the cold March wind. It was the first day of Safety Week, and Christie arrived early to help Jack prepare for the day ahead. She was listening to a particularly fascinating true crime podcast that morning about a murderess in England who poisoned her lover and got away with it. She drove along Lake Shore Drive, admiring the winter sun rising above Lake Michigan. The town was still quiet and rush hour was only just starting. As the sun rose in the sky, big white fluffy clouds rolled off the lake.

She entered the small town of Penakee as the podcaster was explaining that once under suspicion, the murderess tried to blame her husband, who knew nothing of her affair. *Wow*, thought Christie, *people are seldom who they seem*. She pulled up at the plant and walked in, glad to get out of the cold air. She found Jack in the main conference room, setting up for first aid training.

"Hey," Jack said, his eyes shining with excitement. "Thanks again for the suggestion of Safety Week, Christie. I am really excited to get started."

"Of course," replied Christie as she produced a large box of brownies that she had stayed up late to bake last night. Her mother had owned a bakery in England called "Buns-on-the-Wold" in the tiny village of Chipping Natterbury, and she had spent hours learning how to make bread and perfect her scones, cookies, and cakes.

"No Safety Week would be complete without some form of sweet treats," she said, gesturing to the brownies. Jack nodded in agreement. "Remind me again what the plan is for this week?" Christie asked.

"Well, I thought it would get people excited to start with some hands-on training. So, this morning I'm delivering First Aid training, and this afternoon Billy will be delivering Fire Safety training. People can have some fun with it while learning essential skills, too. Tomorrow, we will focus on Ergonomics, and there will be some training around how to set up your workstation correctly. Then some hazard identification activities and prizes and a scavenger hunt for safety items." Jack's excitement was contagious, and Christie glowed with pride that he was taking this seriously and was determined to succeed. In that moment she admired Jack and thought how much she was enjoying working with him.

"That is awesome Jack!" she exclaimed. "I'm thrilled that you have put so much effort into this week and I'm sure it will be a huge success." She turned around to place her laptop down—then uttered a small shriek as she startled and almost fell backwards.

"Jesus Christ, what the hell? Jack, what is, who is?" said Christie, pointing to the manikin lying by the side of the desk.

Jack roared with laughter, "Oh, don't worry about that. It's the manikin for the Cardiopulmonary resuscitation, or CPR, training. You didn't actually think it was real, did you?" Christie had recovered and felt embarrassment come over her as redness crept up her neck and onto her face.

"No" she lied. "It's just for a split second there, it looked so lifelike. I mean, whatever happened to the good old days where you trained with a 'Resuscitation Annie' that looked nothing like a person?"

"Actually, research has proven that the more realistic the manikin, the more that students learn and the more that they feel prepared for the real thing. They use these manikins in the military, and they are becoming more popular in other workplaces now," Jack informed her.

"I had no idea. But that is pretty awesome. I will have to ask my husband if he is familiar with them in the Air Force," Christie said.

"I bet he is. There is a whole market for them now. You can

get older people, babies, children, men, women, different skin colors, hair colors, injuries, and even pregnant manikins that give birth with fake blood to help medical students understand labor. But of course, we won't be going that far today," he said, grinning.

"I guess that's really cool. What about the fake blood though? Do you think that's a good idea? What if some of our employees are a bit squeamish and that puts them off?"

"Well, then they shouldn't be attending a first aid class. It's no place for the faint-hearted. Someone's life could depend upon it."

"Right, but this isn't the Army, Jack. We want to encourage people and engage them in safety this week, not turn them off."

And there it was it, thought Christie, as Jack glowered slightly and fell quiet. It was subtle, but Christie had a feeling that underneath his pleasant demeanor and positive attitude, Jack did not take criticism well. His attitude had altered so quickly. One minute they were laughing and joking, and she was praising him. The next minute he looked like a sulky child who had opened all his presents on Christmas Day and was disappointed to learn that he hadn't got what he wanted from Santa Claus.

Interesting thought Christie. *It was just a simple matter of a difference of opinion.* She was concerned that he would come across as insensitive and make people think negatively about safety, while he thought she was being too soft. It made her think back to the podcast that she had listened to earlier that morning and how people can surprise you. She was about to say something more when Cindy bounded into the room like an excited puppy.

"Oh my God, guys this is so cool," she said looking around the room. "Do you mind if I take pictures throughout the class and upload them to the company social media pages?"

"That's fine," Jack said, apparently recovered and once again at ease and composed.

"This is just marvelous," echoed Sandra entering the room and taking it all in. Christie hadn't seen Sandra look so animated since she discovered that the local herb store had started selling a new range of organic green tea. But it was hard not to be vivacious that morning as there was such a positive atmosphere among everyone.

At nine o'clock the room was full, and Jack began the class. He began by giving an overview of what the first aid class would cover and then explained the main learning objectives. Jack started by describing common workplace injuries, how to stop bleeding and how to apply various bandages. Despite Christie's reservations, the fake blood was used and didn't cause too much anguish. He divided the group into pairs so that they could practice bandaging on each other. He then demonstrated how to deal with choking, burns, and other serious injuries. The group was engaged and attentive, and Christie's heart lifted at how the employees of Belle Corporation were enjoying Jack's class.

They agreed to break for ten minutes and when the group returned, equipped with drinks and snacks, Jack explained that the next part of the class would cover CPR. He unzipped the bag containing the manikin, carefully pulled it out, and laid it on the floor before asking the group to gather around so that they could clearly see his demonstration.

"Oh my God, it's so lifelike," one of the production employees screeched, as she jumped back slightly and raised her hand to her chest. "Seriously, Jack, why did you have to get something that looks like a real person? That is creepy as hell," she said with a little shiver.

"Because it makes it more realistic, which makes the training more effective. Surely it has to be better than those old hard plasticky/rubbery type of manikins that were used for years? Plus, when you see one unconscious body, or even a dead body, regardless of shape, size, skin color, hair color, and so on, they all look the same."

Cindy frowned. 'Really? How so?" she asked skeptically.

"One body looks much like any other body when we're unconscious, because we become limp and heavy, and we have a lighter than normal color. Don't worry Christie was freaked out by it too this morning," he chuckled.

"Wow, that's crazy," replied a young machine operator. "I feel really weird about doing CPR on something that looks like a human."

"Well, how would you feel if you had to do it for real? You would do what you could to save the person, right?"

"That's a good point. Of course I would."

"Let's just try it and see, shall we?" Jack said, in his usual cheerful way of motivating people. Christie's heart sank a little.

To think that she had worried that the fake blood would put people off, when it was the lifelike manikin doing that.

"Actually, I've heard of this before," said a lady with red hair and bright green eyes, named Amy Garsinki. She was the night shift supervisor but had rearranged her shifts this week to be able to attend the training. "My sister lives in Iowa. She's at nursing school in Des Moines and apparently, they were one of the first universities to use these types of manikins for students to learn medical techniques and practice on something that looks lifelike. She sent me some pictures and I thought it was kind of creepy. I never thought I'd get to see one in the flesh though – oops," she said, hand flying to her mouth. "Maybe that was a bad choice of words," she admitted, blushing, as the rest of the group giggled.

"That's really interesting Amy," Jack said warmly. "I read online that some medical schools use them, but didn't know about Des Moines in particular, so thanks for sharing. I believe the military are also using them now, although they weren't doing so when I was still in the Army."

Just as Jack finished talking, a production engineer came into the room late and stopped, rooted to the spot.

"I'm so sorry I'm late, Jack, I got caught up with a customer call about design drawing and - holy cow, is that? Oh my god – is that a real person?" The room erupted with laughter.

"Jesus," he said embarrassed. "It looks so real, like a lifeless body, but obviously it can't be. Now I feel like a moron for thinking so." He laughed along with the others.

"No worries. You can sit down and join in, I was just explaining that it's lifelike to be more effective," Jack said. "Okay, listen up, everyone. When we're starting CPR, it's really important to remember that the first thing you need to do when you discover someone unconscious is to call for help. If someone else is with you, ask them to call 911. If not, then you need to do it. We need to make sure that the trained professionals are on their way as soon as possible. Then grab a defibrillator, of which there are several around the building, and I will show you in just a moment how to use one.

"We will talk now about compressions and breaths. Always start with thirty compressions, because we need to get the blood pumping around the body to deliver essential oxygen to the brain. Everyone following me so far?" The group nodded.

"Great. After your compressions, give two rescue breaths, pinching the nose and covering the mouth completely. Then go back to thirty compressions, then give two breaths. This is the cycle that we are going to keep doing until help arrives. There's only one exception to the rule, and that's if somebody's been drowning, then we can start with the rescue breaths. Everyone got that?" The group nodded again, keen to practice doing this themselves.

One by one, they went up to the front of the room, and following Jack's demonstration of CPR, they completed the sequence of thirty compressions, followed by two rescue breaths. After they had each practiced a couple of times, they found they were more comfortable than they thought they would be with the lifelike manikin. Some of the group even started to giggle and give it a name,

"Oh my goodness this looks just like my uncle Bob, especially when he'd had a few drinks. He does look pretty pale. I guess he knows it's cold outside," a young guy named Martin said, as others around him giggled.

As promised, Cindy couldn't resist the urge to whip out her phone and take some pictures of the training for the company social media pages, and of course she had to take a selfie with the manikin. She immediately uploaded the photos to the company's LinkedIn, Facebook and Instagram account with the following phrases #guesswho'sdoingfirstaidtrainingtoday and #reallifelookingmanikinfreakyorwhat.

"Is that your new boyfriend, Cindy?" asked Billy in a sly, mocking tone, turning around with the hope of having an audience while he made fun of her. Cindy, never one to be easily intimidated, turned and looked Billy straight in the eyes. Without missing a beat, she replied in her strong Southern accent, "Well, yes actually Billy it is. Quite an upgrade from my last one, don't you think?"

As cool as a cucumber, she walked to the other side of the room. She smiled to herself. She couldn't stand Billy, but the opportunity to show her disdain made her feel good. She breathed deeply and relaxed. She knew that he couldn't get away with treating her this way forever. Sooner or later, she would deal with him, and it would stop.

Christie turned away to hide the fact that she was laughing and rather pathetically turned it into an unconvincing cough. She was starting to like Cindy more and more. Billy looked furious and like he desperately wanted to retort but caught Jack's eye and thought better of it.

A couple of hours later, the class was over, and the group were surrounding Jack thanking him profusely for his efforts. They confirmed how much they had learned and demonstrated their newfound enthusiasm for first aid. They took advantage of the free lunch of hot dogs and burgers in the cafeteria and returned to work. Christie praised Jack again for the successful morning. Jack flushed with pride and although he tried to modestly shrug it off, it was obvious that he enjoyed the recognition.

"I really enjoyed it. Hopefully those folks will never need to use it but if they do, at least they are better prepared now," Jack said.

"So, what's with the tension between Billy and Cindy?" Christie asked, once everyone had left and the door was closed. One of Christie's weaknesses was never missing the opportunity to gossip. "There's clearly no love lost there. I had to laugh and admire the way she stood up for herself, but I am also shocked that he would speak to a HR Manager like that. I mean it's disrespectful anyway, but seriously, HR?"

"I know," Jack agreed. "The problem is that Billy is untouchable, and he knows it. One of the old-school types. I mean sure Cindy could get him into trouble, and maybe he'd even receive a warning or disciplinary action, but he would never get fired, and he knows it."

"Really?" Christie asked curiously. "Why's that?"

"It all happened years ago, before I started here. The story goes that there was finance manager working here who embezzled money, and Billy caught her."

"Seriously? How?" Christie asked, with the same thrill she felt when reading one of her beloved detective fiction novels.

"Apparently, she set herself up as a vendor in our system and essentially processed invoices and paid herself. This was years ago, before we had all the checks and balances that we have now of course. Billy got questioned about a supplier of welding gases. Acetylene, I think it was. The price seemed pretty high, and when he looked at the invoice, it was a company he had never heard of or used. Pretty shocking, really, that someone could be so immoral. But Billy helped to catch her. She was fired, of course, and I believe that she is still incarcerated. Ever since then, Billy has been the golden boy at Belle Corporation. He's a smart guy too. What he doesn't know about this place isn't worth knowing."

"Whoa, that's impressive. But why does he give Cindy such a hard time?"

"Oh, Cindy is young and made a mistake. She had an affair with a married man, and he promised her the world. He told her that if she moved here for him, he would leave his wife, and they would live together. That's why she left Oklahoma. Only once she moved here, he lost interest and stayed with his wife.

She was pretty cut up about it and embarrassed. However, the guy was Billy's neighbor, and from Billy's point of view, Cindy attempted to be a homewrecker."

"What? And what about the jerk of a guy?" Christie asked, outraged at the injustice. "He cheats on his wife and he's just innocent in Billy's eyes?"

"Well, like I say, he's the old-fashioned type—you know, a little misogynistic."

"A little?" Christie scoffed. "But how strange that he does something so noble and honorable, like rooting out an embezzler, and then he behaves that way towards Cindy."

"Yes, but just because someone is a good person doesn't mean that they can't behave poorly, too. We are all capable of good and bad," Jack said, in such a matter-of-fact tone that Christie almost felt like she was listening to a sermon in church. Still, she couldn't help agreeing with Jack and admiring his maturity and understanding of human nature.

CHAPTER FOURTEEN

The next day passed in much the same way, with morale increasing among employees as they enjoyed the various safety activities that Jack and Christie had planned. Cindy won the prize for identifying all the safety items on the scavenger hunt. A production employee named Wayne Cartwright won the prize for identifying the most significant hazard, which was part of a machine that wasn't fully guarded and could therefore potentially crush hands or fingers. His suggestion for implementing a mesh guard around the exposed part would eliminate the hazard, while still enabling employees to see the material being fed through the machine.

In second place was another production employee named Emma Beddingfield who had identified a well-known hazard –

a machine whose noise levels reached ninety-two decibels, the loudest of all the machines in the plant. Rather than solely rely upon the mandatory wearing of hearing protection in the area around the machine, Emma suggested a superior control for noise reduction. She proposed that noise-reducing material could be used to cover parts of the machine to absorb vibration and sound. It was simple, inexpensive, and something that Billy and his team could install themselves. Both Jack and Christie had been very impressed that Emma had challenged the status quo and thought of engineering controls above more basic, administrative controls.

Emma's father had worked at dockyards, building ships for the Navy back in the 1960s, and had suffered hearing loss as a result of uncontrolled, noisy environments. She therefore had an interest in the prevention of the same illness for others. She had recently become very interested in the topic and had spent time watching several YouTube videos about hearing loss prevention.

Christie got to work immediately to find a specialist contractor to fit the machine guard that Wayne had suggested, while Jack wasted no time in researching acoustic materials that would be compatible with the machine. Within a week, the guard had been fitted and the sound-absorbing material had arrived. Jack and Billy measured out the material, but to Billy's surprise, when it arrived, he realized that he had ordered too much. As Billy's maintenance shop was very limited for extra space, Jack stored the excess material in the hazardous waste storage area, confident it could be used for similar projects in the future.

The Corporate Safety team were impressed with the success of Safety Week, and Jack had even been told that a promotion was on the cards for him. He was asked to publish his article on the company's internal website to inspire other plants with ideas for safety improvements. Several weeks passed by with no incident, and the atmosphere was one of calm as the plant's productivity flourished, targets were achieved, and employee morale was high.

Then an accident occurred. It came about quite suddenly, on a Tuesday afternoon. Billy had erected a stepladder in Paul's office, which was adjacent to the production floor, and climbed up it to change a light bulb. As he reached forwards, suddenly the ladder swayed and fell to the right, causing Billy to fall with it. Fortunately, he was not seriously hurt— just some minor bruising to his hip and thigh. As many Belle employees were now trained in First Aid, thanks to Jack's recent class, several of them heard the crash and left their machines to rush over and assistt.

Jack was walking around the corner, heard the commotion, and also ran over to help. He told the others they could return to work while he took over first aid duties. He suggested applying ice to the injured area. Billy grunted about not needing ice or any other sort of treatment and pulled himself up onto his feet.

When Jack asked about the cause of the fall Billy replied that he had no idea. Jack asked when the ladder was last inspected, and Billy confirmed that he had completed safety inspections for all ladders that very morning and had noted no defects. Upon closer examination, Jack saw that a screw was loose on the side of the ladder.

"That is impossible," Billy said. "I checked it this morning and nothing was loose."

"Is it possible that when you carried it over here from your office, something could have worked loose?"

"It's not impossible," he conceded reluctantly, "but it's unlikely." Billy shook his head. "You want to know what I think?" he asked, although clearly this was a rhetorical question. "I think someone is deliberately tampering with things in this place. Nothing makes sense, we have "Safety Week", and everything is great. We go back to normal and then accidents start up again."

"But who would do that and why?" Jack asked, shaking his head disbelievingly.

"I don't know. But someone should look into it," Billy retorted angrily.

"I really don't think there is anyone at Belle who would do that, Billy. Also, everyone was hyper-focused on safety during "Safety Week", so it makes sense that we were less likely to have accidents during the week of the event."

Billy shook his head, clearly not listening to Jack. He picked up the ladder and limped out of the office.

"I'll be back with another ladder to finish that job," he called as he went.

Jack found Christie and filled her in on the incident that had just occurred. In the meantime, Billy was making his feelings clear to just about everyone who would listen. By late in the afternoon, he had requested a meeting with Sandra and told her that he thought there was some kind of sabotage occurring at the plant. He cornered Jack and Christie in the cafeteria over lunch and repeated his concerns to them. He saw Daniella outside the boiler room and told her about it.

Furthermore, he reported it to Paul and suggested that Paul should meet with Cindy to start an investigation. He also told numerous production employees, and even threatened to call the corporate leadership team, until Sandra reassured him that it wouldn't be necessary, since there was nothing they could do without proof.

Rather surprisingly, Billy then let the matter rest and didn't mention it again. It was possible that he felt frustrated that no one took his claims seriously and therefore retreated into his shell, but that wasn't in keeping with his character. Initially, he was furious that he was a casualty of a "deliberate" accident. Daniella also seemed restless and agitated. Christie wondered if she had taken Billy's claims seriously and was worried about sabotage. Jack said very little and didn't seem concerned. When Christie brought it up again during their investigation into Billy's fall, he laughed it off and said Billy was known for going off on a tangent and then sulking like a child when no one took him seriously.

Christie decided to walk around the building to check that

the fire exits were closed. Truthfully, she felt like some fresh air after the tension that had been building in the offices all day. As she walked past the maintenance office, she overheard whispers inside. She bent down to tie her shoelace and caught part of the conversation between Billy and Daniella.

"You understand, don't you?" Billy asked. "There is an opportunity here. What is the old saying - a picture tells a thousand words? Well, not in this case. More like a picture tells a thousand lies."

Then came Daniella's voice faintly, "I don't like it. But I agree there may be an opportunity."

A more subtle person might have walked away at that point, but not Christie Hunter. She had no scruples of that kind. Just as she was straining to hear more, Sandra came around the corner, almost colliding with her.

"Goodness, Christie, are you all right?" asked Sandra.

"Oh yes, just tying my shoelace," Christie answered.

"Christie, I noticed that one of the emergency showers was obstructed just now. Someone left a box in front of it, so I moved it out of the way. But it got me thinking about keeping our emergency equipment clear and accessible, and completing inspections to verify that. Do you know if Jack completes them?"

"Not Jack," Christie replied, relieved to move the conversation forward, but secretly frustrated to have lost an opportunity to continue eavesdropping. "I understand that Billy tests the emergency showers every week. I remember him saying that he does it every Monday, because he mentioned it at some point during the Safety Week Scavenger Hunt activity. I believe he does it early each morning to avoid disruption to busy production times."

"That's good to know. Thanks Christie. I'm glad you're getting so well acquainted with us here. We'll certainly be sorry to see you go when your time is up," Sandra said, kindly.

"Likewise," Christie said as she stepped back to let Sandra past. She turned her head back towards Billy's office but noticed that the door was now firmly shut and consequently she had lost her opportunity to hear any more of their conversation.

Sandra left Christie and made her way to Cindy's office for a meeting about recruitment updates. Cindy smiled as she entered. Sandra returned the smile and asked her how she was, to which she replied that she was fine.

"By the way Cindy, before we get started with this meeting, I want to congratulate you for doing a great job with the raffle sale tickets."

"Thank you," replied Cindy, "But how did you know? I didn't think we'd finished selling tickets yet."

"Technically we haven't, but I thought I'd collect the money from the sales completed so far. I went around to everyone's office to collect their takings, and saw that, as usual, you were so organized," she gushed as she gave Cindy a little pat on the shoulder. "You put your takings into an envelope, right? So, I took it and added it to the rest. $200, right? I think we made

$2500 in total," Sandra continued, oblivious to the color draining from Cindy's face.

"What?" said Cindy "You took the envelope from my desk?"

"I did. I hope that's okay?" but before Cindy had a chance to answer, Sandra continued, "Oh, and Cindy, you know me, I'm not really one for telling my leadership team how to do their jobs. But in this case, I would like to offer you some advice. Be careful leaving money lying around, okay? You can't be too trusting anywhere today, unfortunately."

"Sure," Cindy said recovering herself outwardly, while inside her brain was whirring like crazy. If Sandra had taken that money, then what was that cash shoved inside Billy's catalogue? She felt sick thinking that it may actually have been his personal cash that she had taken__*stolen, actually*, she thought, cringing. But no, if it was his personal cash, why was it hidden away in a catalogue? What was he up to?

CHAPTER FIFTEEN

Billy sat at his desk, lost in thought. He stared numbly at the computer screen in front of him, multiple tabs open, ranging from web pages with parts that he needed to order for machine repairs, maintenance orders that were piling up, to emails about attending meetings. He looked around his office trying to focus on work, but his mind was elsewhere.

His office was much like any other maintenance office, with a small section designated for administrative work and the rest resembling a machine shop. Tools, rags, and oil cans were taking up space on the floor. He started to think very carefully about what he had said to others that morning. He knew it was a flaw in his character that he couldn't keep quiet when something important was on his mind. He was concerned that someone really was sabotaging the plant, and he had a pretty good idea who it was. But how could he prove it?

He clicked onto his email inbox and scrolled through his emails, going back to the beginning of the month. Billy was not organized, and he therefore seldom sorted or deleted emails. Despite being chastised for this by Sandra and Paul on a regular basis, he now realized that it had its advantages. Now he would be able to retrieve one email that could set his idea of proving his theory in motion.

He shuddered as he thought about how Sandra's telling him off reminded him of his mother, who always thought she knew best and would only ever call him William in a condescending tone. *But William should have won a scholarship. William should have received the highest grades in the class*, his mother had complained to the school while he stood there mortified. *William should have been given the part of Romeo in the school play. William should have won the sports prize.* He cringed at the thought of it now.

How he wished he could have just grown up in a normal family or had done something like join the Army as Jack did. Still, what was a normal family?

People always asked that question when he complained about his family. *There' no such thing as a normal family—we're all dysfunctional in some way*, a previous girlfriend had said while laughing, and he'd been irritated by how quickly she'd dismissed his point of view.

He hadn't told anyone at Belle Corporation about how he had a master's degree in chemistry. They would only want him to use it, just like his overbearing mother and father. He didn't want recognition. He wanted to fade into the background and be like everyone else. That was the reason he couldn't understand or bring himself to like Cindy. Flaunting herself like that on Instagram and wanting attention. Content to break up a marriage just to be a "somebody", to associate herself with money. It made his insides curdle.

A new email notification popped up on his screen, bringing his attention back to his computer. He scanned the title and saw something about a snowstorm warning. He would read that later. *Snow is hardly unusual in Milwaukee* he thought aggravated. He thought back to his theory of sabotage causing the spate of accidents at Belle Corporation. He was determined, like a dog with a bone, to prove his theory to be correct.

At the beginning of every month, Jack emailed all the managers and supervisors a summary of all accidents that had occurred during the previous month. He tracked lost time incidents, near miss incidents, incidents requiring first aid treatment or more severe medical treatment, work-related illnesses and included various graphs to demonstrate trends in improvements, or not, over the year. Billy quickly glanced over February's accident report. There were the details of Liena Chang's fall in the cafeteria and the flying part ejected from the machine that almost hit Katie's face. He knew his own fall from the ladder would be added to March's report.

Billy made his way to the closet where Daniella stored the cleaning supplies and looked at the floor cleaner. Next to it was a can of machine oil, used for lubricating machine parts. *How strange*, he thought. *That should be with the maintenance supplies, not with the cleaning products.* His team was aware of that, and they were usually compliant with storing chemicals correctly.

Suddenly a thought occurred to him, and he took the lid off the cleaning solution and sniffed it. There was the strange smell that he expected. He couldn't prove anything at that moment though. He quickly looked around before picking up the container filled with machine oil and the bottle of cleaning solution and placed them both carefully inside his jacket. He had laboratory equipment at home and planned to test them.

His next stop was the milling machine. He spoke briefly to the machine operator and examined the machine thoroughly under the guise of completing an additional safety check. He determined that it was clean and in good working order. He concluded that no metal chips could fly out of there, unless someone placed extra chips inside the machine deliberately. He moved on until he reached the ladder storage area. He could see where the screw had been loosened.

Later that night, Billy tested the cleaning solution at home. He had converted his basement into a laboratory and regularly worked on projects there. He sampled the solution and compared it to the ingredients in the machine oil container.

Just as I expected, he thought to himself. Someone had added the oil to the cleaning solution to make the floor slippery to deliberately cause an accident. He reached for a nearby piece of paper and pen and quickly scribbled down the ingredients and his conclusion. Similarly, someone deliberately placed additional metal chips inside the machine where they would fly out potentially injuring someone. In addition, somebody deliberately tampered with his ladder causing him to fall.

I tried voicing my concerns. I went to the boss and told her what I thought, and I went to the new safety consultant and told her about it, and nobody seems to be taking me seriously. It's so typical of them. They say safety is their number one priority but when I trying to alert them to the fact that sabotage is happening right under their noses, they don't want to know. I suppose it's the last thing they would ever think of, and therefore they aren't looking for it, he reasoned. Furthermore, *it seems so uncomfortable and unimaginable that we could work with someone who would do such things, so no one wants to believe it.*

Fine, thought Billy stubbornly. *If that's the way it's going to be, then I will make sure that I benefit from this. I'm not afraid to confront the person who I think is responsible and make it beneficial to me. Yes, I will do that tomorrow.*

Billy cleared up his things in his homemade lab and got himself ready for bed. He thought long and hard into the night as sleep evaded him, which it often did. But when he eventually drifted off, he felt good. He would deal with these things in his own way, and he would make it worthwhile, starting tomorrow.

But the next day did not work out at all the way that Billy had planned. He felt confident when waiting in the hazardous waste room that afternoon, as he sat on an empty oil drum, ready to meet with the person he suspected of wrongdoing. They had agreed earlier that morning to meet somewhere secluded to discuss the situation and come to a permanent financial arrangement. The door suddenly opened, and Billy started unexpectedly, jumping to his feet.

He'd expected to hear the person approaching. He pulled himself together; determined to remain calm and in control. But something about this rendezvous felt wrong. The silent approach, the cold stare from the indifferent face that looked at him now. He thought that the individual would be flustered, hand over some cash and maybe even plead with him to cancel their arrangement.

He swallowed nervously and opened his mouth to speak. But before the words could form, a gun was quickly pulled from the other person's pocket and Billy knew then, in that moment, that this had been a terrible idea. There was no way out now and no way of convincing the person to stop. He had walked into his own trap. As he shook his head and held up his trembling hands, the trigger was pulled and all that remained was darkness.

CHAPTER SIXTEEN

MARCH 2022

Christie jumped at the figure emerging from the door. "Christie is that you?" came Sandra's voice through the darkness.

"Oh Sandra, thank God. It's Billy, he's been shot!" Christie cried.

"What did you say?" asked Sandra, her voice trembling, her eyes as big as saucers.

"Jack and I walked to the end of the building, and we came across his body. He's outside the hazardous waste room. Jack is there now attempting CPR, but I think it might be too late, because honestly, he looked dead," Christie struggled to say the last word. "I'm going to wait at the front of the building so that I can direct the emergency responders."

"Oh my God, how can this have happened? Why would anyone shoot him? Was it some kind of accident?"

"I don't think so," Christie replied. "There was no one else around. Whoever did this left him for dead."

Paul came up behind them making them jump.

"There you are Sandra. I wondered where you got to. Oh, hi, Christie. What's happened? You both look like you've seen a ghost."

Christie quickly repeated the facts, and Sandra and Paul ran off in the direction of the hazardous waste room to help Jack. Christie waited for what felt like forever, shivering in the cold, until finally she heard sirens and saw blue flashing lights. She waved frantically to the driver through the thick snowflakes. They scrambled across the snow as quickly as possible and headed towards Billy. The emergency responders attended to Billy, but their efforts were futile. Christie's heart sank as they shook their heads pronouncing him dead.

Two detectives took the lead in securing the crime. Detective Walker was a middle-aged man with dark hair that was graying along his temples, and he had clear blue eyes. He was kind and thorough in his approach and worked deftly. He was well known in the community, having spent all his life in Milwaukee and at least twenty years working for local law enforcement. His colleague, Detective Albright, was a tall, slim woman with blond curly hair tied neatly into a bun. She also had an adept manner and stood over the body, examining it while Detective Walker exhaled loudly.

"Shot through the chest. Well, I'll be damned. I haven't seen anything like this for years in this town. Billy Carter was a much liked and respected member of the community. Who would want him dead?"

"A random attack, maybe? Some lunatic in these parts? Someone intoxicated? Maybe someone who was at the Shootin' Barrel and wandered over here?" Sandra suggested.

"It's hard to say at the moment," replied Detective Walker. "What the fella was doing out here without wearing a coat is anybody's guess. Seems he didn't plan to be out here at any rate. It's far too cold to be walking around in this weather wearing just a thin shirt."

"Yet he was wearing a hat and scarf, so being outside maybe wasn't entirely unexpected," Detective Albright said. "Maybe he rushed out for some reason and couldn't find his coat, so he just quickly grabbed his hat and scarf."

Sandra shook her head in disbelief, as Detective Albright continued, "So Jack, you and Mrs. Hunter here were the ones who found him, right?"

"Yes," Jack said, looking down at the body in dismay. Billy's lifeless body lay there next to the defibrillator which Jack had found hanging on the wall in the hazardous waste room and attempted to use. They stood behind crime scene tape, and it was difficult for any of them to comprehend that any of this was real. Christie trembled as she recalled how she had run towards the parking lot, made the 911 call, and found Sandra.

"Of course, we will conduct formal interviews, but for now, did any of you see anything suspicious? Anything out of the ordinary? Any idea at all who could have done this?" Detective Walker asked.

"No," Sandra replied. "We have never experienced anything as horrific as this at any of our plants in Belle Corporation. We have had a spate of accidents recently, but nothing like this. Security inside is pretty tight. We have approximately one hundred and fifty employees here, most of whom went home just over an hour ago, following instructions from our corporate team, due to the weather. The only reason we are still here is because we were locking up and ensuring everyone had left."

"And did you see anyone still here?" Detective Walker asked.

"No," Paul answered, and the others shook their heads, concurring that no one else was around. "Of course, it's not impossible that an intruder could gain access to the external premises or even wander over from the Shootin' Barrel, but that's not something we have ever experienced."

"Does anyone know when Billy was last seen alive?"

"Yes, I saw him right before our meeting. He confirmed that he knew we were closing early today, and he looked like he was getting ready to leave. Our meeting was over by three o'clock, so that would have been around two forty-five," Christie verified.

"Hmm…well an autopsy will be undertaken and then we will have a more accurate estimate of the time of death. For now, the information that you've provided, combined with the medical evidence from the paramedics, means that we can give a rough estimate that the time of death occurred somewhere between two forty-five and three fifteen." The group stood there silently, still reeling from what had occurred. Detective Walker continued.

"Okay, well, we will take it from here. We suggest you go home, as safely as possible in this weather, and we will be in touch with all of you for further questioning."

CHAPTER SEVENTEEN

Later that evening Christie sat at the kitchen table with Mike. He had run Christie a bath and had tried to persuade her to eat something. Although she had agreed to the bath, she had refused any food. She sat there now with the faint smell of eucalyptus bubble bath radiating from her skin, her hair still slightly damp, her mind a million miles away. Mike squeezed her hand gently, empathizing with his wife.

Nothing prepared a person for the first time they saw a dead body, and Mike knew from his years in the military that it would be something that would always stay with her. They talked long into the night before eventually going to bed.

The next morning Christie lay wide awake in bed. She had barely slept for more than a few hours, listening to the wind rattle against the house, the sound deep and resonant, vibrating the roof above them. But she knew it wasn't the storm that was keeping her awake. She had too much reverberating around her head.

Slowly she got out of bed and made her way downstairs. She walked towards the patio door and looked outside. Now that the storm had passed, everything looked so still and calm. Thick snow had covered the yard like an enormous white blanket. The trees hung heavy with it; their branches weighed down. The weaker twigs had already snapped off, unable to sustain the weight of the snow or hold against the strength of the wind. Small footprints were dotted across the lawn where an animal, possibly a raccoon, had roamed in the night.

Lola danced around Christie's feet and despite feeling solemn, Christie couldn't help but smile at their adorable dog.

"You don't really want to go outside, Lola. Trust me, you just think you do." Lola barked in disagreement and Christie opened the door. Sure enough, Lola rushed out in a flurry of exhilaration, only to stop running after a few minutes and quickly retreat into the warmth of the house.

"See? I told you. It's cold and you don't like getting your paws wet because you're a little princess," Christie said, teasing her as she reached for her treat jar and indulged Lola in a large turkey flavored treat.

She then padded over to the coffee maker and turned it on when her phone vibrated. She wondered who that could be at six o'clock and what this day would bring. How was one supposed to function after a murder? In the detective fiction that she enjoyed reading so much they all seemed to just get on with their days, but how did it work in real life?

She reached for her phone and saw that it was Sandra

Sorry to text so early but I think Ron Giles may want you to lead an internal investigation into what happened. Clearly the police will lead the criminal investigation, but corporate would like us to do something in addition. Also, I'm currently working on communicating what happened to employees and Cindy is setting up counseling services. Need to work with the media too and ensure that Belle Corporation controls the narrative as much as possible.

Wow, some snow day, thought Christie, sensing the irony of how much she'd looked forward to slowing down for a few days. Strangely, she found herself glad that she had been asked to lead on the investigation. She felt positive that she could help in some way and that she could put her skills to use. *But how I am supposed to start this when we are all snowed in?*

She texted Sandra back. *No problem, I am up anyway. I'm sure none of us slept well. I would be happy to lead an internal investigation. Assuming the police are okay with this, and it doesn't encroach on their work?*

Absolutely, Sandra replied. *You will need to collaborate with them, but I trust you to be professional about it.*

Christie decided that her best course of action was to speak to Ron Giles first to seek clarity about her assignment and then to speak to the police. A brief phone call with Ron confirmed that the senior leadership at Belle Corporation deemed Christie to be the ideal person to lead an internal investigation, as she was impartial and independent. They emphasized the importance of exercising due diligence in establishing how the incident had occurred. They wanted Christie to work alongside the police to determine how such an incident could be avoided again and appreciated that this would take some time to establish.

Christie took a deep breath after the phone call, absorbing the magnitude of the task that lay ahead of her. She knew from years of completing accident investigations that it was imperative to conduct interviews as soon as possible, before people had the opportunity to forget facts, overthink their answers, or falsify statements. She resolved to focus on that first. She would need to talk to the two detectives that she met yesterday and then begin her own interviews.

Feeling better now that she had a plan of action for the day, Christie made herself a cup of coffee and some toast and looked out of the window. The snow was deeper than she remembered seeing for years. The weather forecasters were not wrong about this storm.

Mike appeared and wrapped his arms around her. "How are you doing this morning?" he asked.

"I'm okay," she replied, truthfully. "Actually, Belle Corporation want me to lead on an internal investigation into the, um, incident." She still couldn't get used to saying murder, despite the long discussion that she and Mike had had last night.

"Really?" asked Mike, looking surprised.

"Yes, and honestly I'm glad. It will give me something to focus on, and it means that I'm doing something productive rather than replaying the awful events of yesterday over in my mind."

"That's true. Well, you will make an excellent Miss Marple, darling," Mike said, deliberately trying to keep the mood light-hearted. "I'm going to grab some coffee, get in the shower, then get out of your way."

"You're working remotely today, I assume?" Christie asked.

"Yes, the Commander decided to close the base, except for a few essential personnel, so I'll be upstairs in the office if you need me."

"Thanks honey," she replied, reaching up to kiss him.

She moved over to the dining room table and turned on her laptop when her phone rang again.

"Good morning. Is this Mrs. Hunter?" asked a vaguely familiar formal male voice.

"Yes, this is Christie Hunter," she replied.

"Hello Mrs. Hunter, this is Detective Walker and I'm with my colleague Detective Albright. We met at Belle Corporation yesterday?"

"Yes, of course. Good morning, detectives," Christie said.

"We are conducting interviews with those present at the scene yesterday and would like to speak to you as soon as possible. Of course, we understand that the snow is making travel very difficult today. Would you talk to us via a Zoom meeting, Mrs.

Hunter? It will be recorded, of course, but it would be preferable to a phone call as we be able to see each other on screen."

"Yes, I would be happy to do that. I'm actually available now, if that works?"

"Excellent. If you could provide your email address, then we will get that set up right away." Christie, feeling relieved that she didn't have an embarrassing email address like she had twenty years ago, provided her personal one and as soon as she received the Zoom link, joined the call, curious to learn what the detectives would ask her and how they would feel about her investigating the murder alongside them.

CHAPTER EIGHTEEN

"So, Mrs. Hunter, we understand that you are Mike Hunter's wife, correct? Your husband is a fine police officer. We've worked with him several times on local cases when we've been short staffed and called in help from the nearby Air Force base."

"Please call me Christie and thank you for your kind words about Mike. He was just here actually, but it's a good thing that he's gone upstairs now and doesn't get an oversized ego from the compliments," Christie said chuckling. She was unsure if humor was inappropriate given the gravity of the situation, but neither detective seemed to mind.

"Well pass on my regards to him. So how is it that you ended up at the plant yesterday, and with a murder in the midst, no less? Well, we'll get to all that in a moment. I understand that you're going to be leading on an internal investigation for Belle Corporation?" Christie confirmed that she was. "Just to be clear, Christie, we are the professionals here, and if you find out anything, anything at all that could be useful to us, you must inform us immediately, okay?"

"Oh yes, of course," she said nodding at the camera.

"What Detective Walker means is that collaboration is key to success here," Detective Albright said, trying to smooth over some of her colleague's abrasiveness. "We may not be able to share details with you, but we expect you to share information with us. I know that may not seem like a fair exchange, but unfortunately, that's the way these things go."

"I understand," Christie said calmly. She was smart enough not to argue with two detectives and confident enough in her own skills to know that she would be successful in completing the investigation to the best of her ability. It was hardly her regular line of work, asking potential suspects about a murder investigation, but she was determined to help bring about justice for Billy.

"We will start by asking you to describe exactly what happened yesterday. We have already spoken to Jack this morning and understand that you were with Jack when the body was found?"

"Yes. That's correct. Oh, and if I may ask, how is Jack this morning? He seemed pretty shaken up yesterday." She knew she would speak to him shortly but was keen to know how he was faring, especially after the CPR attempt.

"He is doing okay," Detective Walker confirmed. "He seemed to be a bit hung up about forgetting to use the defibrillator immediately when he started CPR. In fact he mentioned it more than once. I guess he takes the responsibility of first aid very seriously especially as he's the trainer at the plant. But that's what shock can do to a fella. After all he remembered it a few minutes after you left him, so he did his best."

"He did," Christie agreed, already getting the impression that Walker seemed to sympathize with the "fellas" more than the ladies.

As if realizing that they kept getting off point, Walker finally asked, "Can you explain how you found the body and the details surrounding it, please?"

"Of course. The decision had been made by the corporate team to close the plant due to the weather and therefore to send all employees home. Sandra had just received that information and she and Paul informed all employees that they would close early and that they should go home before the weather got worse. She decided to have a brief meeting with the leadership team and I to finalize details around the closure and plan remote work for the next few days.. I was there, as I've been part of the leadership team meetings since I've been working as a consultant for the past three months. The meeting ended and Jack suggested that we check the building and grounds to ensure that all employees had left, before locking up and going home ourselves."

"Why was that?" asked Detective Albright curiously.

"Oh, because apparently some of their employees don't like to leave. You know the type who view work as their life and are sometimes skeptical about weather warnings? We wanted to ensure they had gone home for their own safety. It doesn't bear thinking about how Billy could still be lying there undiscovered if we hadn't done that," Christie said, shivering at the thought.

"Who went on this walk around?" Detective Walker asked.

"Jack and I went outside, Sandra and Paul covered the factory floor, and Cindy checked on office employees."

"And how long did this take?"

"No more than fifteen minutes. Jack and I didn't see anyone, so we assumed everyone had left. We were almost done when we noticed a reddish color liquid leaking from the hazardous waste room. At first, we thought it was some kind of spill, you know, maybe oil or chemicals or paint, but as we turned the corner, we noticed a body and realized it was blood."

"And you recognized it immediately as Billy?"

"Yes, straight away because of his name on his shirt. All production and maintenance employees at Belle have their names embroidered onto their uniform. It was hard to see his face. He was wearing a scarf and hat, and he was paler than usual, of course. Then everything just seemed to happen so fast. Jack crouched down and didn't know for sure if he was dead. I mean he certainly looked like he was, and he wasn't breathing, but Jack wanted to try CPR just in case there was even a remote chance of survival."

"I see. So naturally, as Jack is the first aid and CPR trainer at Belle Corporation, he took the lead?"

"Yes, that's right. He recently taught a first aid class there and was very thorough. He's actually a real stickler for doing everything perfectly –" Christie stopped suddenly, chewing on her lip thoughtfully.

"Christie? Is there something else?"

"No, no, I was just recalling the training that he did with us," she answered truthfully.

Christie frowned, then immediately straightened her face, not wanting to cause any suspicion, although she feared it was probably too late for that. She had remembered something that confused her, but she didn't want to share it with the police yet. She wanted to share it with Mike and get his thoughts, even though she knew he would berate her for withholding anything from the police. But she didn't want to overreact. It probably wasn't important.

When Jack had taught CPR, he was thorough almost to a fault. He insisted over and over again that everything must be done in the correct order, and he had been strict with everyone in the class while observing them practice.

Check the area for danger. She could her his clear voice instructing the group…. well, they had done that with Billy. They had approached the area cautiously not knowing whether to expect a large-scale spill of something potentially toxic…*Call for help.* She had done that just as soon as she had pulled herself together enough to make that 911 call and go in search of Sandra or anyone else who could help. *Check for breathing.* Jack had done that, or at least, she was sure he had, opening Billy's airway and saying that he had to try CPR. *Start compressions.*

That was the part that was confusing her now. Jack had not started with compressions. She distinctly remembered turning around and seeing him crouched over the body starting CPR by giving two rescue breaths. Why? She remembered in class their discussion around how this is appropriate when the victim has been involved in a drowning incident, but clearly Billy had been shot, not drowned. Why then had Jack started with the breaths? That was so out of character for Jack, who was obsessed with following the rules to the absolute letter.

He had also forgotten to use the defibrillator in the beginning, meaning precious minutes were wasted until he remembered. Was it possible that the stress and horror of the situation had caused Jack to panic and forget the correct sequence? Christie had read many accounts of people doing the incorrect thing under pressure. But wasn't it also true that in an emergency your training kicks in, even if you completed the training years ago? People remember things that they were certain they would forget. She had also read that the urgency of the situation, combined with your adrenaline, makes you perform well in an emergency. Still, it was strange that Jack hadn't completed things in the correct order. Was she over-analyzing something that might not be important? She knew over-analysis was one of her flaws.

She was brought back to the current conversation by Detective Walker asking her if there was anything else she could remember, or anything else that she thought was important about the day that Billy died. She replied in the negative. She was determined to explore every avenue for the company's internal investigation. Christie had read enough detective novels in her life to know that even the small, seemingly unimportant things that are observed before, during and after a crime can be significant in solving the mystery. Sometimes even more so than the bigger clues.

But she shook her head thoughtfully. This was not a detective story, after all. It was real life. Her interview concluded with the reaffirmation that she, as an impartial person, would lead the company's internal investigation and work together with the police as appropriate. The detectives thanked her for her time and just as she was saying goodbye, she suddenly remembered something that she did feel comfortable sharing with them.

"Actually, there was one more thing," she said. "After I made the 911 call, I ran to the front of the building to wait for the police and ambulance so that I could direct them to the back of the building. But a few minutes before I got there, when I was by the side of the building, I heard a bang. It wasn't particularly loud and I'm assuming that being so close to the shooting range, it came from there. It sounded very similar to the gunshots that can be heard often at Belle Corporation. I just thought I'd mention it."

"I'm sure it probably did come from the range, but can you be more specific, Christie? You said a few minutes before you arrived at the front of the building, but do you have any idea of the time?" Detective Albright asked as she made a note of it.

"I don't know the exact time, but it was right before I ran into Sandra and Paul at the side of the building. It was a few minutes after I left Jack so if I had to guess I would say around three thirty."

"Okay, thanks Christie. We can check up on that with the shooting range. Thanks again for today and we'll speak with you again soon."

CHAPTER NINETEEN

Following her Zoom call with the detectives, Christie returned her attention to her laptop and set up her own Zoom calls with the leadership team so that she could start her interviews. She began with Jack.

"Hey Jack, I know this may seem a bit strange that I'm interviewing you when we've worked so closely together for the past three months. Corporate have asked me as an impartial, independent person to lead on an internal investigation for Belle corporation. I hope you can understand," explained Christie.

"Really?" Jack, asked looking taken aback. "I'm surprised that they are bothering with an internal investigation given that the police lead on this kind of matter. I mean, after all, it is a criminal investigation, right?"

Oh God, he does mind, Christie thought uneasily. *Oh well, it's not like I volunteered to do it, so he'll just have to be okay with it.* She had enough to think about, without worrying about his hurt feelings. Still, she wished it didn't feel quite so awkward.

"You're right, the police will lead on it, but I think that Ron was keen that we exercise some due diligence. After all, for any severe accidents, including fatalities, there would always be an internal investigation. Clearly Billy's death was not the result of an accident but more of a...," Christie swallowed, "A willful intent for him to die. Nevertheless, it is good practice to interview witnesses and see what we can learn from this, and I'll be working closely with the police to get answers."

For a second Christie wondered if she imagined it as she looked at the screen and saw the look on Jack's face was one of slight resentment because she had been issued this task rather than him.

She noticed that his smile didn't reach his eyes as he said, "Sure, Christie. Whatever you need to do. Whatever you need to ask me, I will be here to help answer your questions and if you need additional help with the investigation, please just let me know." She wished she could have appeased him by asking him to help her with the investigation, but that was not the instruction from Ron, so she knew that she couldn't.

"Thanks Jack, I appreciate that," Christie replied. "Well, I guess I don't need to ask you where you were at the time of the incident given that we were together when we found Billy. Can you just describe to me what you saw and what you did, and I will document your response?"

"Sure," Jack said. "Well, as you know, we were checking the building to see if any employees were outside when we saw something leaking from the hazardous waste room. We walked over to look into it, thinking it was some kind of spill, only to discover Billy's dead body. I checked but couldn't establish breathing, but I wanted to give him every chance to survive and therefore began CPR."

"So, Jack, could you explain to me what you did in relation to CPR?"

"What do you mean?" Jack asked, frowning. "You were there. You saw what I did."

"I did, yes. But could you describe the sequence of events when you administered CPR?"

"Um, well, I think I did exactly what I recently trained everyone to do. I checked for breathing, but couldn't confirm breathing, so started compressions, followed by two breaths, and repeated that cycle. I then realized after I'd sent you to make the 911 call and locate the first responders, that I hadn't used the defibrillator, which of course I should have done.

At that point I had to stop CPR and reach for it. Thankfully there is a defibrillator that hangs up on the wall in there. I was then able to apply the pads, start the defibrillator and continue CPR until the paramedics arrived."

"Thank you for your account, Jack," Christie said, "For some reason I thought that you started CPR with two breaths, and I wondered why, that's all. I mean, not that it really matters at this point, of course. Maybe it is my mistake," she added, careful not to insult him or lose trust.

"Christie, are you criticizing my technique? Are you actually implying that I did CPR incorrectly and that Billy would still be alive if I hadn't?" Jack asked, his eyes flashing defensively.

"Oh goodness, no!" Christie said not expecting her statement to have backfired so monumentally. "Absolutely not. Like I said it was probably my mistake, you know with the shock of everything, it's not always easy to recall stressful events."

"Hmm," Jack murmured frowning, clearly still not entirely convinced, before saying "You know, I really think you've misremembered something, Christie. Like you say, it happens under stress" he added, almost sympathetically. "Starting with the breaths would not have been the correct sequence. Perhaps you forgot what you saw me do."

"I'm sure I did, and as I said, it is of no importance," Christie said although she was certain that she had not forgotten and had just said so to bring the conversation to an end. Christie knew she had an excellent memory, but there it was again: Jack's defensiveness and inability to take any kind of criticism. Maybe he felt guilty because he had been unable to save Billy, but that was ridiculous, Billy was most likely already dead when he attempted CPR. Christie was certain that Jack was lying, and it intrigued her. She felt it was an insight into his personality and pride.

"Well, thank you very much, Jack, you've been really helpful. Oh and Jack, just one more thing - at any point when you were doing CPR, did you hear a noise similar to a gunshot?"

"A gunshot?" he asked incredulously. "No, absolutely not. What makes you think that I would have heard a gunshot?"

"Because I heard something similar when I was waiting for the ambulance. Of course, it's likely it came from the shooting range next door, but I just wondered if you heard anything?"

"No. Honestly between the storm and snow coming down and focusing on CPR, I think I would have barely heard somebody shouting my name, let alone anything else. But you're right that it probably came from the shooting range. We hear them all the time at work."

CHAPTER TWENTY

Christie's next Zoom interview was with Sandra. Sandra looked different from her usual self. She was sitting in a dark room in her house, which she called her consulting room. Christie tried to keep a straight face as she described to her in detail how this was the room she used to contact spirits. Through Sandra's picture on her screen, Christie could make out incense sticks, candles, and a variety of brightly colored pictures hung in the background behind Sandra. Sandra was wearing a black head scarf and a long black floaty top. Christie wondered if she was deliberately in mourning clothes.

Christie asked Sandra to account for the time between the end of the leadership meeting and the time until she and Paul ran over to where Billy lay. Sandra recounted the need to check that employees had left the building and then explained how she and Paul had walked from the offices through the entire production floor, past Billy's office but noticed no one there, so they assumed he must have already left.

"There really isn't anything more to tell you, Christie. Paul and I were together the whole time, and we didn't see any employees who were still on the premises."

"You were together the whole time?" repeated Christie. "But when I saw you as you exited the side of the building via the fire exit door and explained to you what had happened, Paul came up behind you a few minutes later. Remember how he made us both jump?"

"Oh yes. Well, that was because I answered a phone call as we were walking around the production floor and then I headed to the side of the building. I think he was behind me for most of that time, though. Actually, I noticed the door was open, so I shut it to keep the snow and wind out as it was making it hard to hear while I was on the phone."

"So why did you then exit through the door?" asked Christie.

"I was about to turn back when I heard footsteps running and a scream and realized there was someone out there. Of course, when I opened the door again, I saw you on the other side. I think Paul came up behind me just a bit later," Sandra replied.

"Okay, thank you for clarifying that point, Sandra. Is there anything else that you can think of that might be useful for the purposes of this investigation?" Christie asked.

"There is nothing else that I saw or heard, but the whole situation has made me realize that we need to assess our security at the plant. It's difficult to enter the building without a badge, but the exterior isn't so secure. Although we don't know what happened yet to cause this tragic incident, I am certain that we could secure the outside areas better than we currently do. I am already talking to the corporate team about that."

"That's a great point, Sandra. Well, thank you for your time this morning, and just let me know if there is anything else I can do to help."

"Thanks, Christie. We truly appreciate all that you are doing for us."

Christie's next interview was with Paul. She explained the process to him and the format of her interviews and asked him to describe his actions after Sandra announced the early closure of the plant. He seemed uncharacteristically nervous. Clearly being interviewed was not something he was comfortable with.

"Yes, well, it's like I told the two detectives, Sandra and I walked through the production floor and ensured all employees had left, which they had. We checked areas where some may have still been working, including the maintenance shop, but everyone had already gone."

"So, what did you do after that?" asked Christie.

"Sandra and I just started to walk back to our offices, ready to leave," Paul said.

Christie frowned. "Paul, are you forgetting that you and

Sandra exited through a side door, you were actually a few minutes behind Sandra, and that is when you saw me?"

"Oh yes," Paul said, twisting his fingers together nervously. "Well, that's what I meant. We planned to leave the production floor via the side door."

"But you said that you were both walking back to your offices, presumably to collect your belongings. That door isn't the exit nearest to Sandra's office is it, Paul? That's the one at the side of the factory," Christie said, slowly and calmly as one would explain something complicated to a child.

"Well, I know that, of course and that's what I meant, um, sometimes Sandra leaves via that exit."

"Sandra sometimes leaves via an exit on the factory floor, when her office is at the front on the building, near to the front door which leads right out into the parking lot? Why would she walk a good distance in the opposite direction of the front door, if her goal is to get to her car? I mean, I understand you doing that because your office is right by the factory, but Sandra?" she asked, raising her eyebrows skeptically. Paul opened his mouth and closed it again, as if doing a rather good impression of a goldfish. He hesitated, his lower lip giving a slight but not subtle enough tremble, as if about to tell the truth, but then deciding to continue with his story,

"Sometimes she leaves that way because she likes to complete one final check on production, you know, see that machines are running okay and employees are okay, that kind of thing?"

"So yesterday she decided to do that? To vigilantly check on production, even when one hundred percent of your workforce had left the building?" Christie asked smoothly. "I must say, Paul, I'm impressed with your commitment. But what interests me is that isn't what Sandra said. She said you left together through the side door because she heard my footsteps and my scream."

"Damn it," said Paul running his hands through his hair, suddenly looking much older than his years. "Okay, you got me. Christie, please don't be mad or tell the police, but there's something I didn't tell them, and I kept it back for the right reasons. I'm just trying to protect Sandra."

"Sandra? What do you mean protect her?"

"So, here's the thing. We had almost finished our walk through of the production area and we confirmed that no one was still there. Sandra's phone rang and she said she had to answer it, and she needed some privacy. She said when was done she would catch up with me. She was gone for about ten minutes. I like Sandra. She might be a little away with the fairies sometimes..." Christie raised her eyebrows at this last comment. "Okay, a lot of the time, but she is a great leader of this facility."

"Even so, why didn't you feel that you could tell the police about this?" Christie asked.

"I guess I feel a sense of loyalty towards her, since she hired me," Paul replied. "My job here offers excellent compensation Christie, and it meant a lot to both me and my family when I got this job. I owe her a debt of gratitude for that, especially since the pandemic resulted in good jobs being difficult to come by. I also trust her, Christie, and I don't believe she is capable of committing murder. Will I be in trouble for this, Christie?"

Christie looked at Paul and recognized a decent, loyal man when she saw one, but she reminded him that withholding information from the police is serious, and whether he would be in trouble or not, really depends on the outcome.

"What do you mean by that?" he asked, looking startled.

"I mean, if, for example Sandra is the murderer, and you haven't told the police that she was unaccounted for, for ten minutes, it could be grave. But might there have been another reason that you withheld this information, Paul?"

"No," Paul answered, genuinely confused by the question. Although Christie felt sure that Paul was most likely innocent, she felt fascinated and frustrated in equal measure at how dense he was in that moment.

"Well," she said gently. "You see don't you, that if Sandra left you during the walk for, you say approximately ten minutes to make a phone call, meaning that she was presumably alone in that time and without an alibi then, that um…also puts you in the same position doesn't it? You were also alone for ten minutes without an alibi."

CHAPTER TWENTY-ONE

The blood drained from Paul's face and his hands started to tremble as he clasped and unclasped them nervously.

"No, I mean yes, that is correct, but I didn't do anything. I swear I had nothing against Billy. I always liked him, and we got along great. He was a good guy, one of the team here, and I had no reason to kill him," Paul said, without pausing for breath. Christie smiled at him to reassure him.

"Relax, I believe you, Paul," she said. At least she hoped that he was telling the truth, and that he wasn't just an extremely good actor. "What did you do in the ten minutes that Sandra was gone?"

"I just continued to walk around the production areas, checking that people had gone. Then the power went off and the emergency lights came on. I was on the opposite side of the factory to Sandra and when the power went off, I heard a 'pop' noise. It's not unusual for one of our older machines to occasionally make that kind of noise, both when it starts up and shuts off, so I think that's what it was.

I swear I'm telling the truth, Christie. She clearly wanted privacy, and I respected that. She thought she was well hidden behind the large machine near the fire exit, but I could see her feet underneath it when I looked across the floor, so I know she was there that whole time."

"How did you know it was her? Could it have been someone else?"

"It was definitely Sandra because there was no one else around and no one else wears those kind of hippy safety shoes. Remember the power was still on at this point and I could see her safety shoes with the bright pink flowers on them from across the floor.

Anyway, then the power went out, so I made my way to the machine, saw that she had moved and was by the fire exit, which of course was well lit by the emergency lighting, and I made my way towards her."

"Then what did you do?" asked Christie.

"I thought it was best that we walk back to the offices together as the light had diminished, but if she had still been on the phone I was going to say goodbye and head home. As it was, she was just by the fire exit door. I saw her open it and step outside and that's when we met you."

Christie let Paul finish his story and was at least relieved to hear that Sandra had an alibi, assuming everything he said was truthful. However, he caught her attention with something he said towards the end of his statement.

"Paul, let's just go back to what you said a moment ago about what happened when the power went out."

"Oh, you mean how I decided to go and find Sandra once it went dark?"

"No, not that," Christie said. "You said you heard a pop that you thought was a machine shutting down just after the power went out."

"Oh yes, that old thing," Paul said with a chuckle. "Honestly, it's been here since they opened this place. I don't know when we'll ever decommission it and replace it with a newer model."

"Hmmm," Christie murmured, thoughtfully. She tried never to interrupt interviewees during investigations, unless it was absolutely crucial, but sometimes, like now, it really tested her patience when they rambled on. She let him finish and then looked at him.

"Paul are you sure that popping noise was the machine?" she asked.

"Well, what else would it be?" he asked, looking nonplussed.

She looked at him, her face full of concern. "At the time that you heard it, you were on the side of the factory nearest to the hazardous waste room and the location of Billy's death, correct?" Paul nodded in response.

Christie continued cautiously, "Could it perhaps have been the sound of a gun being discharged outside?"

CHAPTER TWENTY-TWO

Christie wasted no time after her interview with Paul in relaying to Detective Walker and Detective Albright what she had learned that morning. She also arranged a follow-up interview with Sandra to determine why she had lied—or at least, withheld information—during her interview about being alone for ten minutes.

"That's interesting information, Christie," Detective Walker said. "So potentially two suspects, each without an alibi. Hmm, definitely something to follow up on today. Well thank you for sharing this with us."

"No problem," Christie replied.

"Christie, a few of the employees we've spoken to mentioned that on the day before Billy died, he had voiced concerns about the recent accidents being the result of sabotage. Do you know anything about that or think that there's any truth in it?" Detective Albright asked.

"Yes, he mentioned it to both Jack and me. It's hard to say. Certainly, the accident investigations haven't been of the quality I would expect for an organization like Belle, so in the absence of other definitive accident causes, it's not impossible. What I mean by that is that there aren't hard facts to entirely dispel that theory. However, Billy was known to be very opinionated about a lot of things and not always reliable. I'll give you an example."

"Please do," Detective Walker said.

"An employee recently had an affair with a married person and Billy spread rumors about how it was all the employee's fault. He only looked at it from one perspective. Of course, the others knew him much better than I did, but I think he was known for outlandish opinions."

"Interesting. We will look further into the sabotage suspicion in case he was right this time, and someone was trying to silence him. People have murdered for less, after all," concluded Detective Walker, grimly.

"Oh, and Christie?" Detective Albright said. "There's one more thing. Something that we discovered that we can bring you in on. It's about that gunshot that you heard after you placed the 911 call."

"Yes?" said Christie, feeling a knot of anxiety in her stomach.

"We checked with the Smokin' Barrel and due to the incoming snowstorm, they closed at one o'clock on Wednesday."

Christie felt her stomach plunge, she felt sick as she said almost in a whisper, "So then, the shot didn't come from there?"

"That's right," said the detectives at the same time.

"So where else can it have come from?"

"We don't know at the moment, but we intend to find out."

"I don't see how it could've come from anyone at Belle Corporation because almost everyone had left. I would have seen anyone with a gun at the front of the building. I mean despite no firearms being permitted at Belle, someone clearly had one to shoot Billy, but this was heard after he had been shot."

"That's exactly what doesn't make sense. By the time you heard that gunshot, Billy had already been shot dead. The Shootin' Barrel had closed approximately two hours earlier and the majority of Belle employees had left for the day. For the handful that remained on site, none of them should have had a gun or reason to use one. They were all getting ready to leave," said Detective Walker.

Christie's mind was racing.

"But what is it that Sherlock Holmes says? 'Once you eliminate the impossible, whatever remains, no matter how improbable, must be the truth.'"

"Meaning?" asked Detective Walker.

"Meaning that one of the people who remained on site—Sandra, Paul, Jack, Cindy, and me—must have fired that shot. It certainly wasn't me."

"We need to look into things further before we can be certain about it where it came from," Detective Walker said in an official voice, gathering some papers on his desk as he spoke, "but that brings us to another interesting point. Miss Cindy Lester. At three o'clock she was checking the offices to ensure staff knew they could leave, correct?"

"That's correct," Christie confirmed.

"Only the interesting thing there, is that none of the office staff got that message from her. In fact, they don't recall seeing her in the offices at all before they left."

Christie's head was spinning with the new information. She scribbled down in her notebook the word "Suspects", underlined it, and wrote Sandra, Paul and Cindy underneath. Immediately she sensed how surreal this felt. Was she playing detective too hard? So, Cindy's time wasn't accounted for, and the gunshot hadn't come from the Shootin' Barrel. She tried to put that out of her mind for now and focused instead on her next call with Sandra.

Sandra answered Christie's Zoom call a little more reluctantly than earlier this morning.

"This is all rather formal, isn't it, Christie?" Sandra asked nervously, as she adjusted her camera slightly and busied herself with getting into a suitable position to be seen on the video call. *She's stalling*, thought Christie.

"I mean two interviews, in one day?" she said, followed by a nervous little laugh. "Have I done something wrong? I've already told you and the police everything I know." Sandra was wearing six gold bangles on her left wrist, and she started to twist one of them subconsciously.

"Not quite everything, though, Sandra," Christie said calmly. "You told me that you answered a phone call when you were walking through the production floor with Paul."

"Yes, that's right. It's not a crime, is it?" Sandra asked with more hostility than Christie thought was necessary.

"Of course not," Christie reassured her. "I'd like to remind you that I'm just here to gather facts. You didn't exactly tell me the truth about that phone call, did you, Sandra?"

"What do you mean? Of course I did. I answered a phone call, as I said previously. What more is there to tell? Do you expect me to share the details of that call? Because I hardly think that is necessary."

"You told me that your phone rang, you stepped away from Paul and walked towards the fire exit door. Then you shut the door to reduce the noise from outside and Paul was just a few seconds behind you. Only that's not quite what happened, is it, Sandra? You answered your phone, walked away from Paul and you were gone for approximately ten minutes, from three ten to three twenty. At some point, after the call ended, you opened the fire exit after hearing me running and yelling for help. Paul then rejoined you. So where were you during those ten minutes, Sandra?"

Sandra froze and for a second Christie thought that the computer screen had frozen, and that Zoom was acting up at a crucial moment. But as Sandra returned to fidgeting with her bangles, Christie breathed a sigh of relief as she realized that the technology was still functioning. Sandra looked down at the desk and it was a moment or two before she looked back up at Christie.

"Okay, I'll tell you the truth but trust me when I say this has nothing to do with your investigation, Christie. What I'm about to tell you, I would like to be omitted from the official report, understood?"

Christie sighed impatiently. "Sandra you of all people, due to your position in the company, know how internal corporate investigations work, and that I can't promise that," she said. She then softened her tone, trying to display some empathy and neutrality. "But if it really has no bearing on this investigation, then yes, I can most likely omit it."

"Okay, well, good," Sandra said sullenly, clearly not used to people challenging her. "I answered my phone, walked away from Paul until I was sure I was out of hearing range, and then actually hid behind a large machine. I'm sure you have probably seen it during your time here, it's the large noisy machine that has just been wrapped in sound absorbing material. Not that it was noisy yesterday as we weren't running it due to material shortages. Otherwise of course it would have been far too loud to stand next to for a phone call."

"Yes, I know the machine," confirmed Christie. "But why did you hide? Why not just return to your office?"

"Because it was urgent that I answered the call. I know I could have sent Paul away, but I wasn't thinking straight, with the factory closure, the severe weather moving in and needing the information that I hoped would be on the other end of this call. I just hurriedly answered it and scurried away. The thing is it was Cindy on the phone."

"Cindy?" exclaimed Christie, completely bemused. "Why was she calling you? She was checking the office areas, right? So had she already left the building when you spoke to her or was she still there?"

"She had finished her checks, and she was calling me as she drove home. Hands free, of course. The phone call was personal, and this is the part I don't want anyone to know about. I'm, well, there's no easy way to say this, so I'll just come straight out with it. I'm in debt. A lot of debt. $40,000, to be exact." Christie used every ounce of willpower to remain professional and impassive, but was shocked, and she was also horrified to see that Sandra had started to cry.

"It was so stupid. I have been so, so stupid," said Sandra, as she sobbed. "You see, it started as little things. I would give $50 here and there to the spiritual groups around town. Then they would host events—you know, Ouija board nights and that kind of thing—and then they wanted money for larger seances and to help people who didn't always get the answers that they wanted from the spiritual world.

Over time it's just mounted up. My husband knows nothing about it, Christie. He's a surgeon, specializing in orthopedics, and he also has a postdoctoral degree in Physics. He's very

scientific" – she said "scientific" as though it was a dirty word—
"and doesn't believe in anything spiritual, so he would be furious
if he knew."

Christ, where did those two meet? wondered Christie, as Sandra
continued on and on about her husband. *If it was a dating site,
they certainly didn't match them well.*

"But Sandra, how were you able to keep this from him?"
asked Christie, when Sandra finally finished.

"Oh, it's been surprisingly easy. We have separate accounts and
I've drawn a lot of the money from my retirement fund, which
he has no idea about, but if he finds out he will be livid. Beyond
livid. So, Cindy put me in touch with our Employee Assistance
Program to connect with a financial advisor who can help."

"Okay, thank you for your explanation, Sandra. And where was
Paul during that time? Did you see him while you were hidden?"

"Yes, I peered around the machine a couple of times and
could see that he was on the opposite side of the production
floor. I think he shut a couple of machines off and then the
power went out. I heard his footsteps coming to find me. I
assumed he was worried about me in the dark, and I could just
make out his figure due to the glow of the emergency lights.

That's when I decided to terminate the call with Cindy. She
verified that she had found an advisor for me and had emailed
the details over so that I could call them at my convenience.
That's the truth, Christie. I never left the production floor or
went outside and neither did Paul."

"At any point did you hear a noise like a pop or a bang or even a gunshot?"

"No, I can't say that I did, but I was so wrapped up in my phone call I may have missed something."

"Thanks Sandra. I really appreciate your honesty, and I promise I will be as discreet about your situation as possible."

"Wow," Christie said out loud as she peeled herself off her chair and shut down her laptop. She shouted up the stairs, "Mike, the workday is over, and I am officially opening a bottle of wine!"

CHAPTER TWENTY-THREE

The local authorities partnered with as many organizations as possible to make a substantial, collective effort to clear the snow. Although it was still piled high on the sidewalks, the main roads were passable the following day.

Despite expectations that the local community would be snowed in for days, some businesses slowly began to re-open. Schools remained closed, but Belle Corporation believed it to be the best thing for employee morale to return to some kind of normalcy. The plant therefore re-opened on Friday. There were a few employees who lived in remote parts of the county who were still snowed in at home, but the majority were able to return to work.

They held a two -minute silence for Billy sometime around

mid-morning, and Sandra gave a speech in memory of him. The police presence on site felt strange but reassuring to employees and made them feel that everything possible was being done to ensure that justice would prevail.

Christie settled into the Visitor's Office, which was now starting to feel like her second home and checked her schedule for the day ahead. She decided to start the day by interviewing Cindy in one of the small empty conference rooms on the second floor.

"Hey Cindy," Christie said warmly, as Cindy entered the room looking nervous. She looked so different from the confident lady who was always ready to pose for a selfie while thinking of the perfect hashtag to accompany it.

"How are you holding up?" Christie asked.

"Not bad, I suppose. I mean I've never experienced anything like this before. It's so shocking and devastating. I still can't believe it actually happened."

"I know what you mean," Christie said sympathetically. "We are all in shock and feeling the same way."

"And what about you?" Cindy asked. "I mean you came here as a consultant to help us to improve our safety programs, and you end up investigating a murder? That's wild. Not exactly what you signed up for, right?"

"No, but I never know what to expect with a new client, and they say there's never a dull moment if you work in safety," Christie joked feebly. "I have investigated fatalities before, but always because of workplace accidents, never murder. Of course, the police are doing the official criminal investigation. I'm just helping Belle Corporation with an internal investigation."

"I understand. So, are you collaborating with the police?"

"I am. Although what they tell me is very limited of course," Christie replied. She wondered why Cindy was so interested.

As if reading her mind, Cindy said, "I'm just wondering how this process works. I don't want employees any more unsettled than they already are."

"No, no of course not, and I know you're currently doing a great job with supporting employees who have been psychologically affected by setting up counseling and grief services. I'm only interviewing those of us who were on site at the time of the murder, and of course most people had gone home by the time Billy's body was discovered," Christie confirmed.

"So, what does that mean?" Cindy asked, with a look of intense concentration on her face. "Someone shot him, then the whole workforce went home as instructed by Sandra and Paul, meaning the murderer conveniently had a reason to leave the premises after committing a heinous crime. He or she left with the crowd, most likely hiding in plain sight.

It could have been anyone. That really doesn't narrow it down, does it? Although I suppose if anything good can come out of this, it means that those of us doing the final checks to ensure everyone had left, aren't suspects, are we? My understanding is that we all have an alibi, and Billy was already dead during the checks. So, it had to committed by someone who left earlier?"

"Not exactly," Christie replied.

Cindy narrowed her eyes in surprise. "Really, how so?"

"Well actually it appears that it's the exact opposite of what you just said. You see, a shot was fired after everyone went home. At first it was assumed that it came from the Shootin' Barrel, but the police have confirmed that it didn't. Consequently, that narrows down the suspect list significantly."

Cindy's eyes were as wide as saucers. "Christie, can that really be true? Okay, I'm just going to come out and say it, okay? Billy and I did not like each other and that was no secret. You can ask anyone."

I hardly need to, thought Christie, recalling them sniping at each other during the first aid training, but she didn't want to interrupt Cindy, so she kept her thoughts to herself.

"But I didn't want him dead," Cindy continued. "Seriously, I had no reason to kill him."

"Cindy it's okay, no one is accusing you of anything. I know you two didn't get along, but there is something I wanted to ask you. When Sandra announced the closure and we agreed to check that people had left, your job was to check the offices and inform any remaining employees to go home, correct?"

"That's right," verified Cindy.

"Only you didn't, did you?"

Cindy paled as she asked, "What do you mean?"

"The office employees said that they never saw you and never got that message from you. So, if you didn't go to the offices, where were you between three o'clock and three-fifteen?" Christie asked.

Cindy frowned. "Christie, whoever told you that has got the wrong end of the stick. At three o'clock I did go around the offices on both floors, but everyone had already left. I ran into the maintenance guys on the way out and they said everyone had already got the message. News travels as fast as wildfire in this place, so I wasn't surprised to be honest. Once I saw the empty offices and realized that everyone had gone, I returned to my own office, got my things together and left via the front door."

"Okay," said Christie, patiently. "So why have office employees said that they didn't see you?"

"The reason that the office employees say they didn't see me is because they didn't. They had already gone. I'm sure the police verified the times, but people don't always give accurate answers or remember times correctly, as you and I both know from the investigative sides of our jobs. Ask the maintenance team and they will validate my story. If you are still not happy, I have a further alibi. I was actually on the phone with Sandra at three ten. I'm afraid I can't give you details of that conversation Christie, as it is of a highly confidential nature, and nothing to do with this investigation." She finished looking slightly exhausted after such an outpour of words.

Christie felt her head buzz with frustration and impatience. This was one of the hardest things about investigations – people passing on information with no basis, no facts, just their own assumptions resulting in valuable time being wasted.

"It's okay, Cindy, I actually know about the phone call with Sandra."

"Oh, okay," said Cindy still slightly prickly.

"And you didn't see or hear anything out of place on your way out?"

"No, I didn't see a soul. The parking lot was mostly empty."

"And is there anything else that you can tell me that might be helpful?"

"Well, everything I've told you so far, is exactly the same as what I've told the police. Only…well, there was something that occurred this morning that I didn't tell them because I didn't think it was important, but now sat here talking to you, I think that it could be more significant for an internal investigation."

Christie groaned inwardly. Honestly, why were Belle Corporation employees so determined to withhold things from the police? Although she remembered she had also initially withheld the small detail of Jack's incorrect sequence of events during CPR. She tapped her foot impatiently but immediately caught herself and stopped, not wanting to make Cindy uncomfortable when she was so close to revealing something that may be important.

"I didn't want to bother them with silly internal politics or HR issues, and honestly, Christie you are so much easier to talk to. You're warm and approachable. They just seem very stuffy and sort of intimidating in a way."

Christie smiled appreciatively. "Thanks Cindy. What is it that you would like to share?"

"On the morning of the murder - oh God that sounds like something from a TV show, doesn't it?" she said, awkwardly. "I mean on Wednesday morning, an argument broke out between Billy and one of our employees who works in the shipping department, named Juan Ramirez. Both Juan and Billy typically didn't work well together, or with others, for that matter, and I was monitoring the situation, as was the shipping supervisor, Juliet Clark."

"It seems as though Billy didn't get along with quite a few people here. What was his problem with Juan?" Christie asked.

"Juan can be quite aggressive and not really a team player. He is responsible for unloading deliveries. Every week the maintenance team send their uniforms out to be laundered to a vendor called Soap Suds, who exchange them for clean uniforms. That morning the clean uniforms for the maintenance team arrived as usual, and they had been unpacked and hung on a rail ready for Billy to pick up."

"So, what happened?"

"Billy came along at nine o'clock, as normal, to pick them up and they were all there except for his. Well, you know how Billy could be, he started criticizing Juan and Juan was very defensive and said he had counted them when they arrived at eight thirty and they were all there. Billy called him lazy and ignorant, and it escalated into a verbal argument, until Paul came along and intervened. Juan came to see me afterwards to explain his side of the argument."

"How strange," Christie commented. "And was the shirt belonging to Billy ever found?"

"Not that I know of. Once the situation was de-escalated, it wasn't mentioned again."

"Is it possible that someone else took it by mistake?"

"No," said Cindy. "I asked the same question and Juan confirmed that no one else had been in the shipping area that morning except the night shift supervisor, Amy Garsinki, before she went home, because she checks all areas before she leaves. Jack was also there when he was doing a safety audit at the shipping dock, I believe?"

"That's right, he mentioned it to me," remembered Christie.

"As I already said, Paul was also there at some point to check that the right number of manufacturing materials had arrived for the day and then helped to break up the argument. But there was certainly no one there with any need to take a shirt – Amy, Jack and Paul don't wear uniforms, so don't they wouldn't have even looked at them. I don't know if this is relevant or if I should have told the police."

"Hmm, that's okay Cindy, I can always let them know. It may be relevant, or it may not, but at least I'm aware of it now."

"There's something else Christie—but don't worry," Cindy said quickly. "The police know about this. I was in Billy's office recently and I found some money, two hundred dollars to be exact, hidden in the strangest place." She told Christie the story about the money hidden at the back of a catalogue.

"That is very odd, but I will leave that to the police to explore further," Christie replied.

Cindy confirmed that she had nothing else to report and the interview ended.

After the interview with Cindy, Christie decided that she could use some fresh air. She walked outside and saw the two detectives opposite the building, just outside the hazardous waste room. She waved and walked over to say hello.

"How's it going, Christie?" called Detective Walker.

"Not bad, and you?" she replied.

"We're working to gradually piece things together," he confirmed. Christie nodded and peered behind the crime scene tape. Something was glittering in the sunlight that caught her eye. She strained to see through the open door but saw that it was ice around the drain underneath the emergency shower.

"That's strange," she said pointing towards it. "Has that shower been leaking while you've been in there?"

"No, why do you ask?" Detective Albright asked.

"Because there is ice underneath it."

"Oh yes, we noticed that and we're working on a forensic analysis, as there was a very faint trace of red inside the ice."

"You mean blood?" Christie asked.

"Impossible to say until we get the results back. Unfortunately, we can't allow you in there Christie. In fact, you shouldn't really be over here at all."

"I understand that," Christie replied. "But what I don't

understand is why would there be a frozen puddle from the emergency shower? It isn't activated unless there is an emergency or it's tested as part of an inspection. Billy used to test them every Monday, but it wasn't cold enough last Monday for the water to freeze. Furthermore, I was in here on Tuesday and there was definitely no puddle, which means it must have been activated since then."

She paused for a moment, concentrating on the puddle. "That puddle is definitely new and hasn't had a chance to melt since temperatures have remained below freezing for the last few days. You said the frozen puddle has a slight trace of red in it. Is it possible that the murderer washed away Billy's blood in there?"

The detectives shrugged, looking intrigued, yet more confused than ever.

CHAPTER TWENTY-FOUR

Christie left the police to discuss the mystery of the frozen puddle and returned to her office. She was surprised to find Daniella loitering around in the corridor. She didn't seem to have any reason for being there, but as soon as Jack turned the corner and entered Christie's office, she followed him inside. *Strange,* thought Christie, *but maybe she's just more comfortable speaking with me if Jack is present.*

Jack began to ask Christie about how the investigation was progressing but stopped when he caught sight of Daniella out of the corner of his eye. She entered the small office as stealthily and quietly as a fox, looking solemn. Christie noticed that her eyes were red as if she had been crying.

"I understand that this whole thing has been a shock for you

Daniella," Christie said, sympathetically. "Can we help you in any way?"

"Yes," Daniella said abruptly. "You see, I was still here when the incident happened."

"What?" Christie and Jack said at the same time, unable to hide their surprise.

"Do the police know?" Christie asked.

"No, I haven't told them yet, because I wanted to tell you first," she replied. *Weird,* thought Christie. *There is definitely something strange going on here.*

"Daniella is it okay if I ask you some questions? I'm leading the internal investigation into Billy's death."

"I understand and yes, it's okay," Daniella said, in a bored tone.

"First of all, can you tell us where you were between two-thirty and three-fifteen?

"I was removing the trash from inside the factory."

"So, you were inside the factory for that whole time? Didn't you get the message that we were closing early?" Jack asked.

"Yes, I did, but I wanted to get all the trash disposed of before I left. I didn't like the thought of it just sitting there for days if we were going to close for the rest of the week. So, I emptied all the trash cans, and I took the trash bags out to the dumpster but that was later, at least…" She looked hesitatingly at Jack. "At least I think it was. I can't be exactly sure of the time. I mean I don't remember."

"It's okay Daniella," Jack said patiently. "You're not in trouble.

We just need to know if you saw anything or heard anything—for example a gunshot."

"But how could I? I was nowhere near the hazardous waste room, I just went to the dumpsters and back inside again and then I went home, so naturally I heard and saw nothing. I was just doing what is normal for me at that time of day and walking around emptying trash cans. Obviously if I had stepped outside, if for example, I was emptying the trash in the offices and had gone down the fire escape to take a shortcut to the dumpster, then, then I may have heard something. Or maybe I would have seen this monster, this evil person, this inhuman thing that could be so cruel as to take someone's life. Then, then perhaps I could tell you more but…" She covered her head with her hands and sobbed. "I can't". They were distracted temporarily by Cindy walking past.

"Everything okay?" she mouthed throw the office window, seeing Daniella in tears. Christie nodded and Jack gave her the thumbs up signal, before turning back to Daniella and saying:

"It's okay Daniella, try not to get too upset, we just want facts."

"But facts are what I tell you, Señor, and now, now you have so much trouble to deal with! Poor Christie has to spend her time on an investigation, and you, Jack, they may blame you! They may say that it's your fault for the workplace being unsafe and then you will probably leave. That's if you don't get fired first," she declared dramatically while Jack looked half shocked, and half amused at the prospect. "It's not fair. You see what I'm saying Jack? I don't know what else to say."

"Calm down, Daniella. I know this is a very distressing time, but you are overreacting. Someone has been murdered and Christie is merely doing an internal investigation. The real criminal investigation is in the hands of the police now. As for me, I have no intention of leaving or getting fired!"

"But do you see what I'm saying Jack?" she asked earnestly. "This could all go so wrong, accusations could fly around this place, oh this terrible, terrible place where we once felt safe to work, but now -"

"I do see what you're saying Daniella. But I am not going anywhere. I will be fine, and you will be fine too, okay? I will make sure of it, I promise".

"Jack, you are so good, always so reliable when there is a crisis, thank you," said Daniella, as she relaxed her shoulders and looked nervously at her feet.

"Yes," reaffirmed Christie feeling slightly baffled at Daniella's emotional outburst. "There really is no need to worry Daniella. If there is nothing more you can tell us, then you are free to go."

"Thank you," Daniella said. "If you need me for anything else I will be vacuuming the offices upstairs. It will be good to get back into a normal routine." She smiled anxiously at Christie and gave Jack one more nervous glance before she exited the room.

"Wow," Christie said, exhaling. "What was all that about? Is she normally so emotional? And why was she concerned that you would be blamed or that you will leave?"

"I don't know," Jack replied, looking nonplussed. "She can

be emotional, which I'm not surprised about, as she was close to Billy. I think she has a tendency to overthink things. She values her job here very much, so maybe she's just thinking about the future and worried about the company's reputation and thinks people may leave and the future of this place could be uncertain. I'd be lying if I said the reputation hasn't crossed my mind too. It's all we can do to keep the media at bay at the moment."

"It's understandable that she's anxious about the future," Christie agreed. "Although it's odd that she said she was on the factory floor the whole time, yet neither Sandra nor Paul saw her. Although they may have missed each other when she went out to the dumpster, of course. But did you also get the feeling that she knows more than she's letting on?"

"Absolutely," Jack said grimly.

CHAPTER TWENTY-FIVE

Jack and Christie agreed that it was time to take a break and go and get a coffee from the cafeteria. Christie would have loved nothing more than to have been able to go to The Cinnamon Swirl and indulge in one their far superior coffees, but for now she knew she would have to settle for the mediocre coffee of Belle Corporation. Still, it was wet and warm, as her mother used to say in England when she had brewed tea to her liking. She was a firm believer that a cup of tea solved everything.

For now, Christie had finished her interviews and planned to spend the rest of the day reviewing her interview notes and start to compile her investigation report. After sipping on his lukewarm coffee from the machine, Jack said he was going to go return to his office and check his emails that would undoubtedly be piling up.

As he rose from his seat, a production employee hurried over towards him and said, "Hey Jack, I just saw a patch of ice outside in the parking lot that hasn't been gritted. The maintenance team must have missed it. Good thing I noticed it, or I could have slipped. Can I show you where it is before someone gets hurt? Of course I'll let maintenance know too, but just thought I should report it, as it's pretty hazardous."

"Sure, thank you for letting me know. I'll just get my coat and gloves first and then I'll meet you out there," Jack Said.

"For sure, you'll need to bundle up. The wind is biting out there," he said.

Christie remained in the cafeteria lost in thought about the case. Amy Garsinki walked in and nodded at Christie as she helped herself to a drink.

"Do you mind if I join you?" asked Amy.

"Not at all," replied Christie. They sat for a while, musing over how terrible the murder was and then, as if recognizing simultaneously that there was a need to change the subject, they began to talk of pleasanter things. The hope that this was the last snowstorm of the season, that spring would soon be on its way, plans for Easter. Their conversation was interrupted by a long, ear-splitting scream from outside of the cafeteria.

"What was that?" Amy asked, sharply.

"I don't know," Christie said, leaping up from her seat "but it sounded like it came from the corridor." They ran to the door at the corner of the cafeteria which lay adjacent to a corridor.

The door opened onto a flight of stairs leading to the first-floor offices. What they saw sickened them. Daniella lay in an unnatural position at the bottom of the stairs, her legs crumpled underneath her.

"Oh no Daniella!" Amy gasped. They rushed over. Christie's mind tried to focus as she struggled to comprehend that this was the second time in a few days seeing a body lay in an unnatural position. Her mind felt like it was shutting down, almost as if to protect her from going through the trauma again. *Please don't be dead* she thought, *please, please, Daniella don't be dead*. With relief they heard her moan in pain.

"Daniella it's okay, you've had a fall. We'll get help, you're going to be fine. Call 911 Amy and I'll stay with her," Christie instructed. "There are cops outside, maybe they can help?"

"Sure, I'll call Jack too," Amy said.

"I just saw him in his office," Cindy said, as she reached the bottom of the stairs breathlessly, and bent down to comfort Daniella. By this time many of the office employees had exited their offices, and a few had rushed down the stairs and were gathering around Daniella.

"Give her some space," Christie commanded. As they backed away, something caught Christie's eye. A metallic object was glinting in the weak winter sunshine that was reflected through the large windows in the corridor. As Christie looked closer, she noticed that it was a gun.

"What the hell?" Christie exclaimed, staring at it. "Okay

nobody touch that gun. Leave it exactly where it is so the police can assess it and take fingerprints." Amy returned with two police officers and Jack. They assessed the situation and retrieved the gun. An ambulance also arrived, for the second time in two days, and paramedics attended to Daniella and prepared her for going to the hospital.

"Someone should go with her so she's not alone. She will probably be confused. I would be happy to do it," Jack said. He was visibly shaken at the sight of Daniella.

"Good point, Jack, but I'll go. You stay here, where you're more likely to be needed. These accidents are getting out of control," Cindy remarked, bluntly.

"No, no, I can go," Jack insisted. "Honestly, I don't have much going on this afternoon and she knows me better."

"It won't make a lot of difference who comes with us," a burly paramedic interrupted. "She has a severe head injury, and after the morphine we've just given her, she will be very drowsy and unable to say much."

"Oh okay, well maybe she would appreciate a female colleague then, Cindy?" Jack suggested.

"Absolutely. I'll get my purse and be right with you," Cindy said nodding towards the paramedic.

Christie slumped in her chair back in the Visitor's office which now seemed to be permanently occupied by herself or the police. She was thinking over what had just happened while the police confirmed that they would get their forensics team to examine the gun and reconstruct the fall to determine how it had been caused.

Detective Walker commented, "This place is unbelievable. I know it's too soon to say what happened, but in light of everything, I find it hard to believe Daniella's fall was an accident. I'd say she was pushed."

"My thoughts exactly," Christie replied, solemnly.

"There is clearly a very dangerous person at work here. Honestly, for the safety of employees, I wouldn't be surprised if they closed until we have caught the culprit. Employees here must be feeling very concerned," Detective Walker concluded.

Christie laughed despite the situation. "It's manufacturing, Detective! They will never recover from that kind of hit to production plus what this situation is doing to their reputation. Trust me, they will not close."

Later that afternoon they received confirmation that Daniella had a head injury and fractures to several vertebrae and had therefore been placed into an induced coma, but she was expected to make a full recovery. Christie was correct that Belle Corporation decided that the Milwaukee plant should remain open. Firearms had never been permitted at Belle Corporation, however, Sandra worked closely with the police to ensure stricter enforcement of their policy, in light of the recent violations.

Christie returned home later that evening and got to work in her kitchen baking raspberry cupcakes with lemon frosting.

"Ooh, yummy cupcakes!" Mike said, as the smell wafted through their house.

"Yes, as you well know darling, baking is my therapy. I need a distraction from all this investigation stuff."

"I totally get it. You know, if it's getting too much for you, you can always quit? We don't need the money that badly, and I'm not sure how safe that plant is at the moment."

"Quit? Come on Mike, you can't be serious? I'm not taking any risks. I'm never on my own there and I'm actually enjoying the investigation."

"Okay, okay, I'm just looking out for you."

"I know and I appreciate that. Actually, I've just remembered that I wanted to ask you something about this investigation." Christie explained how Jack had completed CPR in the wrong sequence and asked Mike if he thought there was anything unusual about it.

"I don't think so," Mike said, thinking it over. "But I would let the detectives know just so they have all the facts. Honestly, it's not uncommon for people to forget things under pressure. I mean, why else would he have done it?"

"I really don't know, it just seemed out of character, given his insistence that the sequence of events must be followed correctly."

"But remember that was is in a training environment. The real world is different, especially in emergencies. You say it's out of character, but you've never seen him in an emergency situation before, so maybe it isn't out of character at all. Maybe he is very confident when teaching, but not so much in reality."

"That's an excellent point. You know, I think I've had enough of thinking and analyzing for one day. Let's enjoy these cupcakes and choose a movie to watch," s Christie said, finally feeling like she could relax after a long, troublesome day.

CHAPTER TWENTY-SIX

Despite forensics results taking a while to be available under normal circumstances, the pressure that Belle Corporation put on the police, combined with Mike Hunter pulling a few strings with his law enforcement connections, meant that the results came back much sooner than expected.

"Well, it's interesting Christie," Detective Albright said a week later, as they sat down to a lunch of hamburgers with Detective Walker. They were in the small conference room at Belle Corporation, but they had ordered lunch to go from The Last Mile Cafe. "The results show that the fingerprints on the gun were Daniella's, and the gun was hers too, no doubt about it. We had our forensics team reconstruct the fall, and it really was an accident. The way she fell was consistent with someone falling backwards after losing their footing on the top step."

"But I don't understand," Christie replied, feeling more confused than ever. "Did someone want to kill Daniella? If so, why not shoot her? And why do people keep bringing guns here? This is a place of work."

"Well people are feeling unsafe right now, and while guns are not permitted at Belle Corporation, clearly people are choosing to ignore the rules. That's why Sandra has asked us to help enforce the policy. With additional checks, it's unlikely that we will see any more guns here."

"I thought Daniella was pushed," Christie continued. "And if so, then maybe the person who pushed her was likely to be the same person who killed Billy."

"I thought so, too, but not according to the evidence," Detective Walker said.

"Did she drop the gun?" Christie asked. "Did someone defend themselves against her? Or was *she* defending herself against someone?"

"These are all questions that we are looking into," Detective Albright confirmed.

Christie and the detectives compared notes on the case and talked in general about Billy's character.

"Billy's parents spoke with us earlier," Detective Walker said. "Interesting couple. They couldn't be more different from Billy. No wonder he kept his distance if he didn't want people to know about his privileged background. They only referred to him as

William and they were the posh type, that's for sure. But as far as they know he has no enemies, no one with a grudge against him. Although I don't know how reliable that information is given that they were pretty much estranged."

"Interesting," mused Christie, although she was not at all prepared for what the detectives revealed to her next.

"There was something they didn't know about their son, though, and it surprised them as much as it did us. It appears that Billy was involved in a drug operation," Detective Walker revealed.

"What? A drug operation?" Christie gasped. "Was that why he was murdered?"

"We can't say for sure at this stage, but it's possible," replied Detective Walker.

"But for someone to come to his workplace on a day when the snow is forecast to be the worst in twenty years, and then shoot him? Isn't that a bit dramatic and farfetched? I mean this is Wisconsin, not the wild west!"

"Ah, but it's not quite as simple as that, Christie," Detective Albright said.

"What do you mean?" Christie asked as she leant forward eager to learn more.

"He was dealing drugs from out of the plant."

"What?" Christie was so surprised and felt so much disbelief that she had to suppress the urge to laugh. "Why would anyone be stupid enough to deal drugs from their place of work? Billy was many things, but stupid was not one of them."

"I agree with you there. But he did it because it was easy and lucrative. Billy had a degree in Chemistry and a lab in his home basement where he made the drugs. We think he was supplying them to someone at Belle Corporation and between them, they hid them on site. We found a large quantity of Methamphetamine hidden in the boiler room and we think that his partnern would take them away and sell them. Really, it's not that surprising." *It is to me* thought Christie *but clearly, I've led a very innocent life.*

He went on to say, "Who is going to go poking around the boiler room? Certainly not the police—unless, of course, anyone became suspicious, but why would they? Most employees here work in the factory. They clock in at the start of their shift, do their work, clock out at the end of their shift and go home. Office staff do the same and stay in their location. Very few would ever have reason to enter the boiler room."

"Daniella…" murmured Christie.

"What's that?" asked Detective Albright sharply.

"Daniella," repeated Christie. "She was often in there, cleaning. You know from the first time I met them I thought something was a bit strange—just sensed it, you know?"

"Just sensed it?" Detective Walker asked, frowning skeptically. "We hear that often in cases. Witnesses try their hand at being an amateur detective and tell us they suddenly get a sixth sense about things. Only we're not interested in that. We only want facts."

"No," said Christie firmly, annoyed at fun being made of her when she felt like she was onto something, "that's not what I meant at all. I was actually thinking that Daniella could have been Billy's partner in crime."

"What makes you think that?"

"It's just that you don't normally see cleaning take place in a boiler room. They are known for being dusty and dirty and full of cobwebs, and having old signs half hanging off the walls, and just generally being worn and dilapidated. But on my first day here there was a sign outside the boiler room door that said 'Caution – Cleaning in Progress'. Billy explained there had been some leaks in there, so I assumed Daniella was in there mopping up water.

But when I saw her come out, she didn't have a mop with her. Yet she was very diligent about putting up the sign and then removing it after she had supposedly finished. To be honest, I wondered if they were having an affair."

"Hmmm, well, I wouldn't read too much into that. Maybe she wasn't mopping but she was doing some other kind of cleaning in there."

"Unless…" Christie said, with excitement. "What if it was some sort of code?"

"Code? Oh Lord, we're not in the middle of a spy thriller, here, Christie,' Detective Walker said in exasperation.

"No, I know that," Christie said, trying her hardest to remain composed. "But what if Daniella was the one working with Billy? He supplied the drugs and put the sign 'Caution – Cleaning in Progress' in place was a signal to Daniella that he had just hidden drugs in there. She then she went in there, collected them and took the sign down to signal that she had got them.

I know Cindy was investigating the nature of their relationship as it was perceived by many that they may have been involved romantically, and they spent time in the boiler room for that reason, but what if it wasn't that at all?"

"My God, what if there is something in that?" Detective Albright exclaimed.

"I know it sounds crazy, but I really think it could be possible," Christie said.

"Okay, well that's all for now Christie. Keep us informed if you learn anything new," Detective Walker said, still frowning.

"Yes sir," Christie replied, as she got up and left the room.

CHAPTER TWENTY-SEVEN

Christie began to sort through the fog in her mind. She felt as though an invisible thread was connecting things together, almost beyond her control.

A gunshot fired after Billy was found dead. Why? That made no sense at all. A missing uniform that belonged to Billy. The emergency shower with a pool of frozen water underneath it that enclosed a faint trace of something red in color, possibly blood. Yet there was no apparent reason why that shower should have been activated as it was the wrong day for testing, and as far as Christie and Jack knew there had been no other type of emergency in that room that justified using the emergency shower.

There was also the matter of the incorrect sequence of CPR administered to Billy, a drug smuggling operation, people lying and withholding information from the police during interviews. Secrets, lies, crimes of serious magnitude. There were things that made no sense. Who had a motive? All of them had the opportunity, except for herself and Jack who had been together and discovered the body.

Christie's head hurt trying to process it all. She climbed into her car and decided to stop at The Cinnamon Swirl for a hot chocolate and piece of vanilla cake on her way home. She felt the need for sugar to re-energize herself. She quickly googled to check if the cafe was open, which she felt positive it would be, as the weather had started to ease, and the snow ploughs had cleared the main roads. Upon confirming that it was open, she drove over, parked up and headed inside, the snow crunching beneath her feet and excitement warming her at the prospect of a hot drink and delicious homemade cake.

She ordered and sat at a table in the corner, lost in thought about the investigation. As she stirred her hot chocolate with one hand, she used her other hand to reach into her purse and pull out her phone. She saw that she had an Instagram notification and when she looked at it more closely, she realized that Cindy had sent her a friend request. She hesitated, not normally being one to accept such requests from clients, but as she liked Cindy, she decided to accept.

Not surprisingly Cindy's feed was full of pictures, and Christie noticed just how often she posted. They were constant uploads throughout the workday, and Christie wondered how

Cindy ever got any work done. Then she froze as she saw a selfie of Cindy with a pale looking man. Why did that photo seem familiar? *Oh, wow* she thought almost laughing out loud, *that was the first aid class and that's Cindy with the manikin, not a person. Damn, I fell for it again.*

Christie remembered how Cindy had taken pictures for the company social media pages but clearly, she hadn't been able to resist uploading one to her personal page too. Then a thought occurred to her that was suddenly so far from amusing she had to hold onto the table in front of her to steady herself. Slowly, she looked at the photo again. *No, it couldn't be. That would be impossible, not to mention insane. Wouldn't it?*

Her thoughts were interrupted by the door opening and a gust of icy wind circulating around the place.

"Christie," said a familiar voice. "What a pleasant surprise." It was Detective Albright, looking slightly weather-beaten and in need of shelter from the bitterly cold wind.

"Hi there," Christie replied. "It's good to see you twice in one day. Would you like to join me? This place has the best drinks and baked goods. It's my absolute favorite. They also sell dog treats, so I usually get something for Lola, my Yorkshire Terrier, before I leave."

"Sure, why not?" she said warmly and took a seat. "So how was the rest of your day? Sorry to talk shop, it's a terrible habit of mine."

"Oh no problem, I get it," Christie said. "It was fine. Most people have now accounted for their actions around the time of the incident. How about yours?"

"Overall, it was okay. Forensics has been typically slow but there were no fingerprints on the body of the deceased and no indications about who may have been responsible for his death. But these types of investigations take time Christie, so don't expect miracles, okay? It's not like crime shows on TV when everything is neatly wrapped up in a bow and the conclusion delivered to you on a plate. In the real world it can be painstakingly slow but make no mistake we will leave no stone unturned. Murder, blackmail, drugs. These things are all rare in this town and it has shaken people. We will restore confidence in our community."

Christie nodded. "Detective, how sure can you be about the time of death?"

"We use several techniques to try and be as accurate as possible, but we cannot be one hundred percent exact, as the accuracy of the estimate depends on many factors," she replied.

"Interesting. So, is it possible that death could have occurred later than you think?"

"It is possible, but I think it would be unlikely in this case. Billy was last seen alive by Daniella around two forty-five. You and Jack discovered the body at three-fifteen, correct? So, it must have occurred in that timeframe. Why do you ask?"

"Okay, this is going to sound insane," Christie said, leaning forward and lowering her voice, "but I have an idea that it may have occurred slightly later."

"Later than three-fifteen? But that is when you discovered the body," Detective Albright said perplexed. "I'm not following. What are you talking about, Christie?"

"I told you it would sound insane. Can we go back to the plant? I want to check the hazardous waste room. Please Detective, can you give me authorization to accompany you inside there? If what I'm thinking is correct there is vital evidence in there."

"Is this to do with that frozen puddle with the smudge of red in it again? Because we're already looking into that. Christie we really can't talk like this in a public place."

"Can we drive in your car then?" Christie asked, impatiently.

"Okay, let's go," she said, clearly still hesitant but willing to give Christie the benefit of the doubt that she had something useful to show her. They carefully walked across the parking lot where more snow was falling and got into the police car.

Just as they reached the car Detective Albright's phone pinged and she exclaimed loudly, "Wow, great news. Daniella is awake."

"Oh, that's wonderful news," Christie replied.

"Yes, it says here that her memory is hazy but she's ready to talk so Detective Walker is heading over to the hospital now. I should go too but I want to take you to the plant first." She started the car and as the heat warmed them up, she turned to Christie and said,

"Christie, there is something I can share with you, but I would ask that this doesn't go any further, okay?"

"Of course," Christie said, rubbing her hands together to warm up.

"I mentioned earlier that the forensics results had been a little slow in coming back to us, however we did get results back from the sample of the red mark within the frozen puddle."

Christie drew a sharp intake of breath. "Oh my God, was it Billy's blood?"

"No," she replied.

Christie frowned. "Who else was injured, though? Who could it have belonged to? Hardly anyone goes in there. Really just Billy, Jack and recently me."

"Well, that's the thing Christie. It didn't belong to anyone."

"What do you mean?" Christie was starting to get an uneasy feeling about where this conversation was heading.

"The results showed a mixture of corn syrup, cornstarch, and both red and blue food coloring."

"What? Was it some kind of paint or dye or something?? Not that I remember ever seeing anything like that when I was there. They mostly store oils and acids."

"Unlikely, although we are of course looking into that possibility. The ingredients that I just listed are mostly commonly in fake blood. Any idea why there would be fake blood in there? Someone's idea of a joke?"

"If it's fake blood, I am pretty certain that I know why it was found in there," Christie replied grimly, "and that is what I want to show you when we get there." Detective Albright took her eyes off the road for a second, turned and looked at Christie in surprise. She hadn't expected such a definitive response.

"Okay, but Christie, I will just say this - the blood in that room may have been fake, but the blood found on the body was real. There is no doubt that it belonged to Billy, okay? An autopsy confirmed he died from a gunshot wound to the chest."

"I understand that," Christie said, nodding.

"Good because, and no offense meant by this, but sometimes people get carried away with theories like the victim faked his death or something. However, I can tell you that certainly isn't the case here."

Again, Christie nodded and replied, "Oh I know that, but I also think I know the link to the fake blood and Billy's death. That's if I'm correct about the things that I want to show you in that hazardous waste room."

Detective Albright glanced at her sideways. "What are you saying Christie?" she asked.

Christie didn't miss a beat.

"I'm saying I know who killed Billy."

CHAPTER TWENTY-EIGHT

Christie stood in the center of the same conference room where the leadership team had assembled several weeks ago on that fateful day to discuss the early closure of the plant due to the snowstorm, the day that would always be remembered by them all as the day Billy was murdered.

She noticed that even, or maybe especially, in times of crisis, everyone still sat in their usual places around the table. Maybe people were comforted by the sense of familiarity. Sandra and Cindy sat to the left and Jack and Paul to the right. *We are creatures of habit, after all,* she thought. If it hadn't been for the police circling around the building like sharks in the ocean, it would have felt like a normal day. Production operations were up and running again, the snowstorm had passed and although it was still unbearably cold outside, the sun was shining.

"What are we all doing in here?" Paul asked.

"Waiting for the police. They want to speak to us all and actually so do I," Christie said.

"Well, this is absurd," retorted Paul. "We've already answered their questions. They can't detain us here. We have rights. We should get lawyers if they want to speak to us again. We have work to do. I'm not guilty. None of us did it. We all worked with Billy and liked him. I'm going."

"Sit down," Christie said sharply. Everyone turned and looked at her in surprise. They had never heard her use such a fierce tone. "No one is going anywhere until the police get here. We may have all worked with him, although I'm certain that not all of us liked him, but one of us in here killed him."

"One of us in here killed him?" Cindy asked in disbelief. "Oh please, who gave you authority to hold us captive? I'm sorry Christie, I like you, I really do, but you don't even work for Belle Corporation." After Cindy's outburst, Paul clearly felt confident to continue venting his feelings.

"What is it with safety people always thinking they can take the lead, play the police officer and command others? Or is it that because your husband is a police officer, you think that makes you one too? I suppose you know who committed the murder?" he asked sarcastically.

"Yes, yes that I do," Christie said calmly, despite the tension that was clearly spreading around the room.

"Okay. Let's just calm down everyone, okay?" Jack said, diplomatically. "Christie is not trying to command anyone to do anything. Let the police speak to us when they get here and I'm sure we'll soon be out of here and back to work."

"Oh, you think so, do you?" Christie replied coldly, turning to face Jack. At that moment Detective Walker and Detective Albright arrived and sat down. Neither were happy about Christie concluding her investigation in this manner, which they considered to be far too dramatic and not her place to do. However, they had reluctantly agreed to it and had promised they would be there to help her.

As soon as the detectives sat down, Christie began. "I have spent three months working with all of you and have had the privilege of observing many things. First, very few people here are as they seem. Cindy, you kept secrets about your past and why you really moved to Milwaukee until Billy revealed the truth and spread rumors about you." Cindy squirmed uncomfortably in her chair. "You and Billy did not like each other, did you? He knew about your involvement with a married man, a neighbor and friend of his no less. When the relationship went wrong, he used it to taunt you, didn't he?"

"Yes, I made a mistake, and thanks to him everyone at the plant knows about it, but that doesn't make me a murderer! I didn't kill him to get revenge or silence him, if that's what you think? It was too late anyway. Everyone knew by then!" Cindy exclaimed hysterically, looking horrified.

"Sandra and Paul, it was looking concerning for you both for a while when you, Sandra disappeared during the time of death leaving both yourself and Paul without alibis. However, I think we have cleared that up now." Sandra and Paul exchanged uncomfortable glances but said nothing.

Christie continued, "Daniella isn't here to speak for herself, as she is recovering in the hospital, but many people suspected there may have been a romantic affair between her and Billy. It was no love affair, but they had a good reason to be together on a regular basis. They were running a drugs operation together."

"What the hell?" Jack exclaimed, as Paul said at the same time "Is she for real? A drug operation between Billy and Daniella? Well, now I've heard it all."

Christie nodded and continued. "Billy, who had extensive knowledge of Chemistry, made the drugs and provided them to Daniella who sold them outside of work."

Sandra looked as perplexed as the others in the room. "Billy had extensive knowledge of Chemistry?" she repeated. "But even so, how did they manage a drugs operation right under our noses?"

"Oh, they had a remarkably simple yet clever system," Christie answered. "When the door signs 'Caution - Cleaning in Progress' hung on the boiler room door it meant that drugs had been dropped off and stored in the boiler room. When the sign was taken down it meant that the drugs had been collected. Money was recently found by Cindy in Billy's office-"

"Wait," Cindy interrupted. "Was that money something to do with the drugs?"

"Exactly," replied Christie. "When Daniella paid him his cut, he stashed it away carefully and took it home in small quantities so as not to arouse suspicion. Oh yes, there are quite a number of secrets in this workplace."

"Well, that sounds extremely suspicious to me. Daniella must be the one who killed him!" Jack said, looking shocked but also triumphant with his conclusion.

"Really, Jack? Why? If you are working with someone to store and then pick up drugs, to sell them at a later date, and all is working well, why would you want them dead? It was lucrative and successful," Christie replied.

"I don't know," Jack answered, looking totally confused by it all. "Maybe she had had enough, maybe she wanted out?"

"But that is clearly not the case. Perhaps *your* motive is stronger? Perhaps Billy discovered some secrets of yours?" Christie continued.

"What? Okay I think we're all getting a bit carried away and should leave this to the police," Jack said, looking slightly exhausted by all that had been said in a short space of time. He looked hopefully at the detectives, as if might intervene and stop Christie, but they remained impassive.

"Really, you sit there so calmly, so unfazed by it all," Christie observed in amazement.

Before Jack had a chance to respond, Cindy asked in a small

voice, "Christie, are you suggesting that Jack murdered Billy? That can't be possible. He has an alibi. You were with him when the body was discovered. Remember?" She looked at Christie as if worried that she'd gone slightly insane. "The way you described the angle at which Billy lay...well it was the picture of death itself."

"No, Cindy, I saw what I was meant to see," Christie replied. Everyone stared at Christie in astonishment. Even the detectives couldn't help but be caught up in the suspenseful atmosphere, despite already knowing the outcome. "I saw a picture indeed. An interesting choice of words there, Cindy. A picture tells a thousand words, or in this case, tells a thousand lies. Actually, those were Billy's words the day before he died, and I will explain how he correctly identified the picture that was painted. Let me remind you all of the first thing that Jack did when we discovered the body."

"I can tell everyone myself, I'm sitting right here," Jack said rather sulkily.

"No, I want to share my account, thank you Jack. Well, he supported the head, which had a hat on top and a scarf around the neck, and he said he wasn't sure if he was dead but wanted to try CPR anyway. So, he immediately knelt beside the body, gave two breaths and then started chest compressions. Does anything strike you as odd about that sequence of events?" Everyone looked puzzled. Jack glared furiously at Christie.

"I've got it!" Cindy said like a child that has proudly come top of the class in a quiz. "When Jack taught the recent first aid class, he said that you always start with chest compressions and then give two breaths. The only exception is if the victim has been involved in a drowning incident...which this wasn't..." Her voice tailed off.

"Precisely," Christie remarked. "Jack who never puts a foot wrong, who is known for being meticulous and proud of training first aid so thoroughly, in the correct sequence. So, upon discovering Billy's body, why did he perform CPR in the wrong sequence?"

"I wasn't even aware of it. I just forgot under pressure, and honestly, does it really matter at this point? The guy is dead, and it is now apparent that CPR wouldn't have saved him anyway, so why are we in here debating the correct technique?" Jack said, hardly pausing for breath as he spoke so fast.

Christie laughed despite herself. "Well, I'm glad we agree on something, Jack. You are right. CPR would not have made a difference. No, it would not have saved him. Not at all, given that when you knelt over the body and appeared to carefully protect the head and began with breaths it was all to conceal as much as possible of the face. You needed to hide the fact that the body you were holding was not a body at all, but the manikin from your first aid training!"

"What?" cried everyone in the room in unison. Sandra looked as though she was going to faint, Cindy gripped onto her but whether it was to steady Sandra or herself, it was impossible to say. Paul's eyes were wide, and he looked around the room in disbelief.

"You said yourself Jack during first aid training that 'when you see one unconscious body or even dead body, regardless of shape, size, skin color, hair color etc. they all look the same'. A strange comment to make, yet true in this case."

"What on earth are you talking about, Christie?" Jack asked.

"Oh, this was a crime so carefully and meticulously planned, Jack, and you almost got away with it. You staged the death of Billy. You dressed the manikin with an identical uniform which you took from the shipping department and padded it slightly to resemble Billy's shape. You were the one who insisted that the leadership team checked that the building inside, and particularly outside, before everyone left. Why?"

"To ensure that all employees had gone home."

"No! Because it gave you an excuse to find the body while maintaining an alibi."

"But there was no guarantee that Jack would be the one to check the area outside. What if Sandra and I had volunteered to go outside, leaving Jack and yourself to check the production floor?" challenged Paul.

"Very unlikely, though, isn't it?" Christie countered. "People will gravitate to the areas they know best and the people they are responsible for. Even if that had happened, Jack is a persuasive person and would have argued the point, to ensure he had the opportunity to check the outdoor area. As long as he wasn't alone, that was all that mattered to him.

You see, it was essential he was with someone when the 'body' was found so that he had an alibi. He knew that he was the one to be more comfortable with administering CPR and that the other person would prefer to go and seek help. While the alibi was gone, he disposed of the manikin and killed the real Billy during that time, while it was thought that Billy was already dead."

"Look, Christie, this is all very Hercule Poirot, but where is the real proof that Jack is guilty?" Paul asked.

"I will continue," she said. "Jack had no real reason to be in the shipping department the other day. One of the advantages of working in Safety, right? Safety personnel have authority to go anywhere on site, without question, to check conditions, procedures etc. The roof, the server room, the hazardous waste area, shipping and receiving, offices, the factory floor, boiler rooms, parking lots, gardens, you name it, we can always say we need to check something in relation to safety. Rarely does anyone ever question it, or verify that we are actually doing, what we say we are doing.

Jack was there under the pretense of completing a safety audit, but his real purpose was to go through the clean laundry and take a shirt that belonged to Billy to ensure it had he had a shirt with Billy's name visible in preparation for his manikin. The detectives upon arriving at the crime scene commented that it was strange that Billy was wearing a hat and scarf but no coat."

"That's correct," Detective Walker corroborated. "We wondered why Billy would be semi-dressed in the cold weather. Well, simply because a coat would have hidden the name embroidered onto his shirt. Jack wanted to ensure the name was clearly visible to his alibi so there was no question of who the victim was, while the hat and scarf would help to conceal the manikin's head. As lifelike as the manikin looks, Jack couldn't risk his alibi suspecting that it wasn't a real person." Jack shook his head but said nothing. He was confident to challenge Christie, but uncertain of the detectives.

Christie continued. "I checked the SharePoint and there is no record of a safety audit taking place in the shipping department on that day, because that was not his intention in being in the shipping area that morning."

"Oh please, give me a break," said Jack, rolling his eyes. "This is pathetic, Christie. I mean, really? That's the evidence you're going on? That I didn't upload a stupid audit form to the SharePoint? Who says I didn't? I was probably still working on it when you checked."

But Christie was undeterred.

"How ironic, that while you were supposed to be improving safety, you were accessing areas to do exactly the opposite. I should have known from the first day I met you here and saw you playing the hero on the side of the road at that accident. You told me that you administered first aid, but the police confirmed that there were no injuries that day. You just wanted to be a hero. The same reason that you locked me into the hazardous waste room one day. You knew that Billy was in the area, and I would suspect him and then of course, you would come to the rescue and again, look like a hero. All these things were part of your plan."

"That's an interesting point," Paul said thoughtfully. "You do like to be a hero, Jack."

"Yes, just like when you sent me to get help while all the time looking like the hero and performing CPR on your manikin." Christie said. "You deliberately wanted me out of the way so that you could hide the manikin behind the metal panel in that room. You therefore did not ask me to pass you the defibrillator, which you made a big thing out of acting remorseful and forgetful later, a simple thing that I could have done and should have done. But your emphasis was on sending me away to the get help."

Jack let out a deep sigh and looked pityingly at Christie. He said gently, "Christie are you okay? I'm actually worried about you. These obscene things you are accusing me of just aren't true. They are in fact ludicrous." He looked around the room, attempting to gain support. But the others looked at him doubtfully.

"Don't even think about denying it," Christie said, "because Detective Albright and I broke into that metal panel earlier today. You pretended not to know about the panel or to be in possession of a key to that panel on the day that I discovered it, but you had a key all along and were planning to use it to hide evidence of your crime. We broke into it this afternoon. We also found Billy's coat, because of course the real Billy did go outside dressed appropriately for the weather. But you took his coat off after you killed him and hid it with the manikin and your gun behind the metal panel in the wall in the hazardous waste room."

Sandra looked around in shock and dismay before saying, "But none of this makes sense. Why would you do this Jack? And in such a horrid manner. There's still something that I don't understand. Why was blood found on the opposite side of the room? And why was the emergency shower activated?"

"An excellent question Sandra," replied Detective Albright. "As Jack placed the manikin into the metal panel, some of the fake blood that he used for the chest wound, dripped onto the floor. He then panicked, realizing that there was blood on the opposite side of the room, where it can't be explained. So, he activated the emergency shower to wash it away. Only you weren't quite as thorough as you thought, Jack."

She now stared at him, making him feel uncomfortable. "There was a trace of fake blood left on the ground and with the temperatures being so cold, the water froze almost immediately, enclosing that red color within the frozen puddle on the floor. Forensic analysis determined that it was fake blood, which led Christie and I to put the pieces of this puzzle together."

Jack suddenly went from looking uncomfortable to slightly insane, as he began to laugh hysterically. "You can't prove anything," he said between outbursts of laughter, "This is a set-up. You're just trying to pin this crime on someone and for some unknown reason you've picked me. I'm the real victim here."

"I think we all know that's not true Jack," replied Christie. "After you had hidden the manikin, you reached for your gun, most likely also hidden in the secret metal panel and waited for the real Billy to arrive and then you shot him dead, putting the real time of death around three-thirty. You had arranged to meet Billy because he'd blackmailed you as he knew you were deliberately staging accidents to look like a hero. You arranged to meet in the hazardous waste room where you would pay him for his silence. Only you had no intention of paying him, did you? Your only intention was to silence him for good."

Cindy gasped, "Blackmail? Oh, Jack, how could you? This is all so wrong, you're just evil."

"Oh yes, this was evil and very clever indeed," Christie continued. "You told Billy that this would be the perfect place to meet because no one else accesses that room. Due to the recent noise-reducing project you were working on in the factory, you stored excess acoustic material in there. Ironically any safety professional worth their salt would know that hazardous waste areas should be free of excess material. Although you had a strong motive didn't you Jack? With the hazardous waste room suitably sound proofed, no one would hear the gunshot, or at least it would significantly reduce the sound."

"Except it was heard by both you and I, wasn't it Christie?" Paul asked, remembering details of that afternoon. "Although it was more of a pop or a muffled bang due to the acoustic material absorbing most of the sound. Yes, very clever indeed."

"So, then you just grab the defibrillator from the wall, attach the pads to Billy's chest, the real Billy that is, and continue with your futile CPR attempts?" Sandra asked, looking disturbed.

"No!" Jack exclaimed, defensively. "Why would I do any of this?? What motive would I possibly have for killing Billy? What nonsense is this about staging accidents? My job is to prevent accidents, so why would I deliberately stage them?".

"Ha ha," Christie said. "The motive is as I have already stated. Billy worked out that you had deliberately been sabotaging equipment to cause accidents. You always want to be the hero and administer first aid, take charge of the situation, and bask in the glory of being the person to fix problems. Maybe something that goes back to your childhood, where you were devoid of praise and recognition from your parents."

"It's true," Detective Walker confirmed. "When we searched Billy's home, his lab for drug manufacturing in the basement wasn't the only thing we discovered. Billy was something of a Chemistry genius and he had run some tests to determine if his suspicions were correct. He sampled the floor cleaning solution and detected that machine oil was present. This was most likely because it had been added to the solution to deliberately cause a slippery surface when the floors were mopped.

He also made notes about metal chips deliberately being added to a milling machine to cause parts to eject and a ladder being tampered with to cause instability. It looked as though he was beginning to investigate some of the accidents from last year too, but of course he didn't get that far. He also noted that at every accident Jack was always present. There was never an occasion where an accident occurred and Jack didn't rush to the scene, take charge of the situation, apply first aid and suggest ideas to make things safer. He was onto you Jack. He knew about your desire to play the hero."

Jack shook his head, "Clearly none of you believe anything I have to say so what's the point in me saying any more?" he muttered under his breath.

Christie continued, "What you didn't realize was that during this time when we were all convinced that everyone had gone home due to the weather and subsequent closure, someone was still around. Daniella. When her memory returned after her accident, she gave an account of what happened to the detectives. On the day of the murder, she had just finished collecting all the trash from the offices and was taking it out to the dumpster when she saw, from a distance at the top of the fire escape, Jack in the doorway of the hazardous waste room.

Of course, she didn't question it at first because, like everyone else, she had heard the story about how he had found Billy's body. However, Billy had already told her that he suspected Jack of sabotage. I overheard them talking about an opportunity, of course meaning an opportunity for blackmail. Remember that they both had an interest in making extra money where possible. Then when Billy died, her suspicions that he had already blackmailed Jack were confirmed."

"But why would Daniella want to kill Jack? It seems so out of character for her?" Cindy asked, scrunching her face up in confusion.

"She felt she had nothing to lose, and she hated you Jack for murdering her friend. She wanted revenge, so she blackmailed you too, very discreetly and cleverly in a cryptic manner during her interview with us both. Only she didn't really want your money. No, she planned to kill you in exactly the same way that you killed Billy. She didn't care if it was in the light of day, at her place of work crawling with police officers, because in her mind she'd already lost everything. Her best friend and her much needed additional source of income. She hinted at you in front of me that she knew you were the perpetrator and implied that she wanted something in return for her silence. She knew that you would want to get rid of her like you did with Billy."

"Yes, it was a very clever ruse indeed," Detective Walker commented. "She lured you upstairs and pointed the gun at you. You didn't dare to carry your gun with so many police around, but you were too quick for her. You doubted that she was serious and grabbed the gun from her hands, and in her surprise at your actions, she toppled backwards and fell down the stairs. You couldn't be seen with the gun, but neither could you risk firing it, so you quickly threw it down the stairs after her."

"But if that's true, why weren't Jack's fingerprints discovered on the gun?" Paul asked.

"Once again Jack got lucky there," Christie replied. "Minutes before this took place, an employee reported that there was a patch of ice in the parking lot that hadn't been covered in grit. The employee wanted to show Jack where it was located. Of course, this involved going outside in the snow and therefore wearing outdoor clothing including gloves."

Immediately after reviewing this hazard, instead of going

straight to the maintenance team to tell them about it, Jack went upstairs to see Daniella. So, when he snatched her gun from her -"

"He was wearing gloves when he handled the gun," Cindy finished the sentence, seeing things more clearly now.

"So, his fingerprints were never left on there," added Paul.

"Exactly," Christie replied.

"When you appeared on the scene minutes later, you insisted that you went in the ambulance with her for fear that she would talk, didn't you Jack?" Christie said, turning to look at him. "However, you soon relaxed when the paramedics confirmed that she was drowsy and unlikely to say much."

"You evil bastard," Cindy said.

"I could have finished her off," Jack said clenching his fists, his face contorted and ugly. "I *should* have finished her off. You bitch," He pointed at Christie, glaring. "I just wanted to help people and be recognized. If I had been promoted already, I would never have needed to hurt anyone."

"Oh please," Paul said, rolling his eyes. "You're sick, Jack, sick, you know that?"

"It was Billy's own fault that he got himself killed. He shouldn't have gone poking his nose into things that didn't concern him. He was so sure of himself. I had to silence him. You're all so hypercritical sitting here judging me, when the truth is that none of you really liked him anyway."

"So? Not liking someone, is hardly a reason for killing them, Jack," Sandra said.

Suddenly Jack jumped up and tried to bolt towards the door, but he was no match for the two detectives.

"You can't arrest me, I'm a Safety Manager!" he pleaded, in desperation.

"Yeah, that's not a thing," Detective Albright replied, looking almost bored of Jack's futile attempts to withhold some dignity, while she handcuffed him and led him away.

The others remained seated at the table, still in shock at all that had passed before them in this room.

"You know, there's one thing that still doesn't make sense to me," Sandra said. "Billy figured out that Jack was staging accidents, right? So, he took the opportunity to make some money out of it by blackmailing him. Only it didn't work out for him at all; I mean, he paid the ultimate price with his life. So, when Daniella guessed what happened and of course was devastated by the loss of Billy, why in the world would she go and attempt the same thing? She knew by then how dangerous Jack was and surely, she must have realized that to also blackmail him was incredibly perilous, not to mention just stupid! She could have got herself killed too! Why not just go to the police and report it?"

"As I said, I think she felt she'd got nothing left to lose," said Christie. "I think by mentioning it in front of me, the way that she did, hinting that she knew something, she was showing Jack how serious she was about threatening to expose him. She was playing with fire, but she loved Billy, maybe not in a romantic way, but he was her dear friend. Billy was caught totally off guard, remember? He expected Jack to begrudgingly hand over money and that it would be a bargain between them, but he never expected that Jack would silence him, murder him."

"I see what you mean," Sandra said, slowly absorbing the information. "Daniella knew better. She knew exactly what she was getting into, so she went prepared. She knew that she couldn't threaten him alone in case he was concealing a gun and killed her like he did with Billy, so she did it in the safety of your presence during an interview."

"Exactly," Christie replied. "Then she knew she could casually drop into conversation, where she would be after the interview, and she knew that he wouldn't be able to resist finding her as soon as possible. That's when she brought out her gun. But he was too quick for her and as he reached for her gun she stepped backwards and fell."

"Ironic really that her fall was the only genuine accident that occurred at Belle Corporation since you've been here," Paul said.

"That's true," Christie replied. "As Daniella fell, office employees reporting hearing a scream at ten-thirty and went running to see what was happening. Jack knew that he couldn't risk being caught holding a gun, so he threw it down the stairs after her and ran but Cindy and at least two other people saw him." The group all sat there numb, trying to process all the information they had just heard.

"This whole thing is wild," Cindy said. "Do you think they will make some kind of movie out of it?" They all turned to her before she held up her hands defensively. "Joke, it was a joke, okay?" The others shook their heads at her but couldn't help but laugh, welcoming a little light relief into this otherwise somber day.

Ron Giles called to congratulate Christie on her discovery and thorough investigation. Her time at Belle Corporation had come to an end. With Jack permanently out of the way, Christie was confident that their safety record would improve, and things would return to normal eventually.

Later that evening, Christie and Mike celebrated by having dinner at a restaurant overlooking the lake with Detective Walker and Detective Albright. Christie let them laugh and joke and exchange police stories while she lost herself in memories of the investigation. She was looking forward to having more time to read her favorite crime fiction books and watch her favorite detective shows, where there was safety in knowing that the story wasn't real and would usually have a happy ending.

EPILOGUE

THREE MONTHS LATER

Christie and Mike strolled along the beach hand in hand, watching the waves of Lake Michigan lap against the sandy shore as Lola ran along the beach barking at the seagulls, thoroughly content with this beautiful summer's day. They had decided on an impromptu road trip heading north from Milwaukee to Door County and planned to sample the finest cheese, wine, beer and ice cream available. The day was warm and humid with mild relief in the form of a gentle breeze. Midwestern summers were a stark contrast to midwestern winters.

They turned the corner to see a woman teaching a young boy how to fly a kite. As they got closer her shape looked familiar, but her laugh was more natural and relaxed than Christie remembered.

"Cindy?" Christie called out. Cindy stopped and stared, then relaxed into a smile.

"Christie, how nice to see you. What are the chances you would be here this weekend? This is my nephew, Dexter. My sister's son. They're visiting from Oklahoma for the weekend."

"Hi," Christie said warmly. "This is my husband, Mike."

"Nice to meet you, Mike. Dexter, say hello".

"Hello," said the young boy shyly. "Auntie Cindy, can we try again please?" he asked as the kite drooped down, tails floundering.

"Absolutely, honey," Cindy said, looking at him fondly.

"Well, we won't keep you Cindy, but it's great to see you looking so well," Christie said..

"Thank you," Cindy replied. "It has been an eventful time, but I've been promoted and will be moving on again, this time to a foundry in Amarillo. I'm really looking forward to it."

"Wow, from Wisconsin winters to the Texas heat. Sounds wonderful Cindy, you deserve it. Good luck," Christie said, kindly.

And with a wave farewell, they continued to amble along the beach. Sometimes bad things happen to good people and sometimes good things happen to bad people. But sometimes, just sometimes, the right things happen to the right people, at the right time. Jack's trial date was set, and it was rumored that he would get a life sentence. Sandra had resigned and was enjoying spending time with her family, now that their finances were getting sorted, one step at a time.

Paul continued to work at the plant and provided much needed stability for employees. Daniella made a full recovery from her injuries and had been charged with her involvement in the drugs operation. The Milwaukee plant had hired a new Safety Manager, a pleasant lady who relished the challenge of building the reputation back up again, and everyone knew that the plant would pick itself up again and still be a cornerstone in the city.

"And what about you darling? What will your next adventure be? No more sleuthing, I hope?" Mike asked. Christie laughed and gripped his hand tighter. She had been terrified and pushed herself further than she knew she could go, but a part of her had enjoyed solving the mystery.

"Who knows?" she answered honestly. "A part of me craves the tranquility of England after recent events."

"Me too," agreed Mike, "What I wouldn't give for a cup of tea looking out onto those gorgeous green hills. It would be great to visit Jacob, too, and I'm sure your brother would love to see us."

"Maybe. But I also feel like just getting away and going somewhere crazy like Las Vegas," Christie said, thoughtfully.

"Las Vegas? I didn't have you down as a gambler," Mike replied, laughing.

"Haha, you know what I mean, just somewhere totally different from here, you know? Somewhere out west, it doesn't have to be Las Vegas, maybe Reno. Somewhere for a nice break."

Mike smiled and nodded. "Anywhere with you would be just fine. I think a well-deserved break is exactly what we need."

ACKNOWLEDGEMENTS

I would like to thank my loving partner Brian, without whom I would never have written this book. Your encouragement and faith in me made it possible and I love you. An acknowledgement must also be made to Hunter, our adorable little Yorkshire Terrier, who spent many hours by my side as I wrote this book. I would also like to say a special thank you to my mom who has always encouraged me to reach for the stars. I enjoy our many conversations about our shared love of literature.

Thank you to my editor Bryn Donovan for helping me to fine tune my debut novel and thank you to my designer David Prendergast for making the book look great. Finding you both at www.reedsy.com was extremely helpful. Finally, a big thank you to all my readers. I am so grateful to you all for taking the time to read this book. I hope you enjoy reading it as much as I enjoyed writing it!

Printed in Great Britain
by Amazon

54571539R00128